Whispers of Trust

Whispers of Trust

SARAH DAVISON

XULON PRESS

Xulon Press
555 Winderley Pl, Suite 225
Maitland, FL 32751
407.339.4217
www.xulonpress.com

XULON
PRESS

Unless otherwise indicated, Scripture quotations taken from the Holy Bible, New International Version (NIV). Copyright © 1973, 1978, 1984, 2011 by Biblica, Inc.™. Used by permission. All rights reserved.

Paperback ISBN-13: 979-8-86850-296-5
Ebook ISBN-13: 979-8-86850-297-2

Dedication

First, I want to dedicate this book to God, the true Author of life
and the reason there is a story to tell.

Secondly, I would like to dedicate this in honor of my grandpa,
whom we fondly called "Kitty Grandpa" because of the
cats around the barnyard.

Proverbs 3:5-6

"Trust in the LORD with all your heart and lean not on your own understanding; in all your ways submit to him, and he will make your paths straight."

Prologue

One year ago

Eleanor Wilson crouched behind the brush, trying to quiet her breathing. At the sound of footsteps, she crouched down even more ignoring the poking of the bush's prickly pins. She could make out two sets of legs through the greenery. The men on the other side simply stood there. Listening, watching, waiting.

After a mumbled conversation, they finally headed south. When they were out of sight, she sighed in relief. Pulling out her phone, she checked the tracking device. She was about a mile away.

She figured she was close when she again stumbled across the pair patrolling. Saying a quick prayer for protection, she pocketed her phone and set off in the opposite direction as the men.

For the next stretch, bird calls and the soft rustling of animals scurrying across the forest floor accompanied her. As she continued through the wooded area, she couldn't shake the eerie feeling that had been with her since this morning, but still she pressed on.

As she neared a fork in the path, she drew her phone out again. She was close. Quietly, she slipped it back into her hidden pocket and veered right. When she rounded the corner, she saw an opening tucked into a hill. It must be the cave she was searching for.

Eleanor took a moment to survey her surroundings. Nothing stirred. Slowly, she crept forward, ears perked for the slightest movement. She stayed along the tree line until she reached the cave's entrance. Only, it wasn't much of an entrance, more like a child-sized hole. Not for the first time, she was thankful for her small stature.

Kneeling, she pulled a flashlight from her knapsack. Taking another glance around, she tentatively stepped out into the open. Hearing nothing, she ventured out even further until she was standing in front of the cave's opening.

Bending over, she shined her light inside. Satisfied nothing was going to jump out at her, she laid on her stomach and wormed her way into the hole, the flashlight gripped in her hand. She pulled herself forward inch by inch.

Seeing the tunnel widen ahead, she crawled with renewed energy, nearly exclaiming in delight when it revealed a cavern tall enough to stand upright. Straightening to her full height, she swept her light across the space.

Walking around, she searched the ground, walls, and nooks and crannies for clues. When she reached the left side, something caught her gaze. Crouching down, she peered behind a rock. Yes, something was definitely tucked underneath!

Heart racing, she placed her flashlight on the ground and lifted the rock, grunting at its brute weight. Dumping the rock beside her, she saw a piece of paper shoved into a quickly dug hole the size of a man's fist. Grabbing the paper, she shook the dirt free and opened it, her eyes scouring the words before her.

Getting closer. Cave was cleared out. Couldn't have been moved far. Will track the surrounding area then head to the meeting spot. Target is getting antsy. Be careful.

Leaning back against the cave wall, Eleanor sagged in relief, thankful her husband hadn't been caught. When he went off the grid a week ago, she had feared the worst. But this note soothed her worries; she would recognize Andrew's handwriting anywhere.

Focusing again on the message, she contemplated its implications. It appeared they were getting closer to finding the evidence needed to put their target behind bars. Just the thought filled her with satisfaction.

Stuffing the note into her secret pocket, she brushed the loose dirt back into the hole and returned the rock to its place. Picking up her flashlight, she headed back the way she had come.

She squinted when she reentered the sunlight. Not wanting to linger, she quickly retraced her steps to the fork in the path and headed in the direction of the meeting spot.

Her anticipation grew the further she went. Each step brought her closer to being reunited with her husband, delivering the good news to her brother, and hopefully seeing their target in prison soon.

Chapter 1

Present Day

A knock drew Emery Wilson out of her revere. Placing her bookmark inside her latest read, she uncurled from her position and walked hesitantly towards the door. Taking a breath, she turned the handle. Her heart raced at the sight before her.

It's okay, she told herself. *It's not the police.*

Gripping the door for strength, she looked at the stranger, willing herself not to take a step back. "Can…" she cleared her throat and tried again. "Can I help you?"

"I hope so," the man replied, giving a small smile. "My name is Mr. North, and I am looking for Miss Wilson."

Emery studied him. He stood nearly a head taller than her own 5'4". She guessed him to be in his mid-forties. Despite his graying hair, he appeared to keep up his physical physique. His demeanor was friendly enough, yet something in his eyes gave her pause.

"May I ask why you are looking for Miss Wilson?"

Mr. North held out his hands in a placating manner. "It's a matter regarding the young lady's uncle."

Uncle? She knew, of course, that her mother had a brother, but she had never met him. He was just a name. She didn't even have a face to put with it.

She bit the inside of her lip, noticing the man was waiting for a response. Despite everything, a sliver of curiosity urged her onward. "I'm Miss Wilson."

Seeing him reach into his jacket, Emery took an involuntarily step back shielding herself with the door. When she saw him remove an envelope, her shoulders relaxed.

"I have a letter that explains everything. If you have any questions, here's my card with my number."

She began to reach for it but hesitated. "How did you know where to find me?"

"Your uncle wished to contact you, so he hired me to locate you since I work as a private investigator." He pulled a badge out of his inner jacket pocket to show her.

It certainly looked official, Emery thought, watching as he put it back.

"I only wish I had located you sooner," he continued. "I figured offering to deliver the letter in person was the least I could do."

"What do you mean?" she questioned.

He nodded towards the envelope still in his outstretched arm. "I think it would be best for you to read this first and take time to process everything. Afterwards, I will do my best to help you in any way I can."

Slowly, Emery closed the gap and grasped the letter, unable to shake her uneasiness.

Mr. North dipped his head. "I'll leave you to read the letter. Have a good day, Miss Wilson."

With that he turned and started down the walk. Emery's gaze followed him as he got into a black sedan. She continued to look in his direction even after the car was out of sight.

What have I done? she thought. Emery glanced down at the envelope in her hand. Should she open it now, or wait until her friend Anna came home? If she did it now, then she wouldn't have to wonder anymore. On the other hand, it might be easier to open it with the comfort of a friend nearby.

Torn, Emery stepped back inside, shutting the door and leaning back against it. Closing her eyes, she took a deep breath. Against her will, her mind drifted to the past. To a time when she felt scared and alone.

She shook her head, pushing the memories away. It wouldn't do any good to dwell on what couldn't be changed. Opening her eyes, Emery steeled herself and tore the envelope, breaking the seal. Heart hammering, she pulled out the letter and unfolded it.

> To Miss Emery Wilson:
>
> Due to the recent passing of your uncle, Mr. James Adler, the matter of his business and estate, located in Rhode Island, falls to you Miss Emery Wilson, daughter of Mrs. Eleanor Adler Wilson his closest kin and heir. Until your arrival, your uncle arranged for his business manager, Mr. Richard Finley, to oversee the business and estate. The address for the estate is listed below.
>
> Regards:
>
> Mr. Fredrick Jameson, Executor for Mr. James Adler

How could this be? The little Emery knew about her uncle was that he left home at eighteen, and her mom had never seen or heard from him again. How could he have known he had a niece? What did this all mean? Emery lowered herself onto the couch, her mind a daze. What was she going to do?

The sound of an incoming text broke through her mental wandering. Checking her phone, she saw it was Anna saying she was on her way home. Emery relaxed. When Anna got home, she could help her sort everything out. She just needed to keep her mind busy until then.

⸺⧓⸺

Hearing the door, Emery jumped off the couch. Finally, Anna was home!

"Hey," Anna called, hanging up her jacket. "Sorry I'm a little late. The café had a last- minute rush, so I stayed to help."

"That's okay," replied Emery, fidgeting with her hands. She waited for Anna to finish taking off her shoes.

"What were you thinking for dinner?" asked Anna, straightening. "I was thinking…" She paused. "What is it?"

Emery couldn't help a small smile from escaping. "You know me so well."

Anna smiled in return. "I've known you since second grade and you haven't changed much."

Emery supposed that was true. She had been quiet in school and normally kept to herself. Then one day Anna blazed into her life and had been a constant ever since.

"Come on," Anna said, motioning towards the couch. "Tell me what's bothering you."

Taking a seat beside her, Emery tried to bring her thoughts into order. "To be honest, it's so crazy I don't know where to start."

"Start at the beginning," Anna said, folding one of her legs underneath her.

"Well, when I was reading earlier this afternoon, someone knocked on the door. I opened the door to find a man I've never seen before asking for Miss Wilson."

"Really, what did you do?"

Emery shifted, readjusting her position. "I wanted to shut the door, but a small part of me was also curious, so I listened to what he had to say. And you wouldn't believe it…he said my uncle hired him to find me."

"Wait, your mother's brother that apparently disappeared?"

"I wouldn't say disappeared. My mother said one day he just left and never looked back."

Anna leaned forward. "So…this uncle suddenly wants to be part of your life now?"

"Not exactly," Emery said, tracing the pattern on the top of the couch. "The letter said he had passed."

"Oh," Anna reached over. "Are you okay?"

She shrugged. "I guess so. I mean, I didn't know him."

Anna gently squeezed her arm before removing her hand. "He was still family though. That counts for something."

"I suppose," Emery replied. "But that's not even the craziest part."

"What could be crazier than your long-lost uncle reaching out?"

"The letter also said I was heir to my uncle's business and estate in Rhode Island." Emery paused, waiting to see her friend's reaction.

Anna stared at her, dumbfounded. "Wait, hold on," she said, waving her hands. "You're saying this uncle you have never met left you everything?"

Emery nodded.

Anna leaned back, her arms flopping against her sides. "Wow, what are you going to do?"

"I don't know," she replied. "There's just so much I don't understand." She straightened. "One, how did my uncle learn about me? Two, why did he name me his heir? And three, could I really just pack up and go to Rhode Island?"

"But going might be just what you need."

"What?"

Anna sat up. "Think about it Em. The best place to look for answers to your questions is the place where he lived. Maybe there's clues at his place or the people there might be able to help."

"I don't know," Emery answered, biting her lip. "You know I don't like traveling."

"I could go with you. I would be with you every step of the way."

Emery shifted. "There's just so much we don't know."

"But that's how we'll start to know, by going."

"You almost sound excited by all this," said Emery wearily.

Anna smiled. "Maybe a little. I can't deny I've always craved adventure, but this trip is about you." Her friend studied her. "What do you think, Em?"

"Give me the night to think about it," she replied. "It's a lot."

"I understand, take your time. The decision is up to you."

Emery smiled. "Thanks."

"No problem," Anna answered, pushing up from her seated position. "Now, I'll go start dinner and then I want to see the letter."

Emery watched as Anna made her way to the kitchen, feeling calmer yet anxious at the same time. It was a relief to get it off her chest, but the problem still hovered over her. She was curious to learn more about her uncle, but the whole situation was odd.

Had he reached out to her knowing he didn't have much longer? Did he know what had happened to her parents a year ago? All this time she could have had family with her, but now she was back to zero.

Feeling her chest begin to tighten, Emery started taking slow, deep breaths. *It's okay*, she told herself. *You're not alone. You have Anna.*

You also have God, another part of her answered.

Emery tried not to shy away at the thought. She knew God was always there, but she had grown distant since she lost her parents. Eventually, she had gone back to church and started reading her Bible again, but lately it felt like she was going through the motions. She knew she needed to go deeper, to dive back in. But she wasn't ready.

Now, with her world turning upside down again, she felt lost. Where Anna saw possibility and adventure, she saw looming unknowns. She thought about praying, but part of her wavered. Would it do any good? Who was to say this time would be any different.

When she heard Anna's call from the kitchen that dinner would be ready soon, she gladly embraced the opportunity to leave her unwelcome thoughts and questions behind. For now, she would set the table and enjoy a meal with her friend. Everything else could wait.

After getting into her pajamas, Emery perched on the edge of her bed. The evening had been a nice distraction, but now she was left alone with her thoughts. Since the letter arrived, the things she had tried so hard to forget, to push down, now rose defiantly to the surface.

She gripped her head between her hands, tears leaking through her fingers. Her chest shook in quiet sobs. Why was this happening? She had already lost her parents. Why was God asking even more from her?

Reading the letter earlier was like reopening an old wound. It was a stark reminder of all she had lost – her parents and now an uncle she hadn't even known yet couldn't help feeling a twinge of loss for. Why? What was the point of reliving everything?

Emery jerked up, needing an outlet. She wanted to scream, hit something, anything to feel better. She wanted to fight back but couldn't. She wanted answers, but instead was left with why.

Why had God taken her parents? Why had she inherited an estate and business so far away? Why couldn't things run smoothly?

TRUST ME.

Emery turned her head away from the thought, crossing her arms.

I don't see the point. I prayed for You to bring back my parents, but You didn't. Fresh tears streamed down her face. *I've seen You heal people over the years and open doors for others. You could have saved my parents.*

Emery bowed her head as she sat down, the fight going out of her. *It just hurts so much.*

Crawling to the head of the bed, she sank into the pillows, curling her arms around her stomach. She pulled the throw blanket over her, letting the softness warm her, wishing it was a hug. Releasing a slow breath, she closed her eyes and simply laid there, allowing the quiet to soothe her.

Before long, her breathing became regular, and her eyes grew heavy. She snuggled deeper into the pillows, pulling the blanket tighter. A small sigh escaped as she let the burdens of the day fall away, sleep pulling her gently into its fold.

Chapter 2

Emery

Nearly twenty-four hours later, Emery still couldn't wrap her mind around everything. It was like being dropped into the middle of a maze without a map. No matter which way she turned, she found herself lost. Had her mother lied about not being in communication with her brother? If so, what else wasn't true?

To think everything she had grown up hearing about him might be false was overwhelming, creating cracks in her structured life. Trying to push such thoughts away, she busied herself with getting ready, hoping the routine would calm her.

As she finished, she set her brush on the counter and took one last glance in the mirror. The same nose, ears, lips, and cheeks filled her face. The same chestnut colored hair fell just past her shoulders matching her ordinary brown eyes. Except nothing was ordinary about her life now. Sighing, she turned from her reflection and headed to the living room to see if Anna was ready.

Entering the room, she didn't see any sign of Anna. Needing something to keep herself busy, she began straightening a few things that were askew. A couple of minutes later, she heard Anna coming down the hall.

Fluffing one last pillow, she turned to find Anna wearing the emerald dress that complimented her complexion nicely and lent her copper curls a fiery appearance. The ensemble seemed to bring her friend's personality to life.

In comparison, her light blue skirt seemed to lack the luster of Anna's. It was better fit to blend into the background, which suited Emery just fine. Noticing the time, she grabbed her Bible off the end table and followed Anna out the door.

As they climbed into the car they shared, Emery tried to still her tumbling thoughts, yet her mind seemed unable to fixate on anything else. She cracked the window as they drove along, imagining the wind taking away all her worries.

They continued the drive in comfortable silence until they reached their destination. Seeing the steeple, Emery hoped she would find an inkling of peace within its four walls. She mounted the steps alongside Anna and entered the church, doing her best to display a calm demeanor. They took their usual seats in the middle section. Leaning back against the pew, Emery's thoughts drifted to yesterday.

Noticing someone in her peripheral vision, she turned and saw it was Mr. North. Had he followed them? Was he expecting an answer about the letter? Emery's heartbeat increased. She wasn't ready yet.

"What is it?" Anna asked.

Emery faced forward again. "I just saw Mr. North."

"Who?" Anna turned to look behind them.

Emery grabbed her friend's arm. "The man who dropped off the letter," she whispered.

"Oh…" Anna replied, sneaking another peek backwards. "What do you think he's doing here?"

Emery shrugged, but before she could respond she heard the pastor greet the congregation. She forced herself to focus on what the pastor was saying, but a small part of her kept wanting to look behind her.

Rising with the congregation for the opening hymn, she kept her gaze forward, letting her voice join the throng of fellow worshippers singing praise to their Heavenly Father. As they started the second verse, the words seemed to jump off the screen at her.

> "Sometimes mid scenes of deepest gloom
> Sometimes where Eden's bowers bloom
> By waters still, over troubled sea
> Still 'tis His hand that leadeth me."

Emery closed her eyes as the words of the song "He Leadeth Me" washed over her. Troubled sea was an accurate description of how she was feeling. Her world had turned upside down and she felt disoriented, tossed like the waves of the sea. The song was a reminder that no matter where life took her, God would be with her, leading and guiding.

She thought back to her prayer the night before. Instead of a plea for help, she had lashed out in frustration and anger. Was she wrong to have done so? Opening her eyes, she looked around. Some sang with tears in their eyes and others lifted their hands toward heaven. They sang with such heart, such conviction. What was she missing?

She looked down. She didn't feel strong or confident. Instead, fear and uncertainty plagued her. They had been her constant companion for so long she wasn't sure how to feel anything else.

Hearing the chorus of the song, she glanced up, reading the words as those around her sang. All the while her mind raced. Could she trust God after everything that had happened? Her hands gripped the pew in front of her, her knuckles turning white.

As the song ended, she sat down and tried to push such thinking from her mind. She wanted to do better, truly, but this recent turn of events regarding her uncle was opening wounds that hadn't fully healed. Despite her best efforts, her parents' absence was a hurdle she just couldn't overcome. It continually halted any forward progress, leaving her wondering if she would ever feel whole again.

Emery was still pondering the pastor's message as she descended the church steps. She heard Anna talking to someone a few feet behind her, so she stopped to wait. She saw Mr. North approaching and glanced back. Seeing Anna heading her way, she breathed a sigh of relief. She turned just as Mr. North drew to a stop in front of her.

He dipped his head before speaking. "Good morning, I was wondering if you've had a chance to read the letter."

Emery swallowed; her words trapped in her throat. She felt Anna draw up beside her. Her muscles relaxed enough to nod her head yes.

"Let me start then by saying how sorry I am for your loss," Mr. North replied. "Were you close to your uncle?"

She shook her head from side to side, the words still under lock and key inside of her.

Mr. North studied her briefly before continuing. "Have you given any thought whether you will go to Rhode Island?"

Thought about it? She hadn't been able to think about much else! But anytime her mind wandered in that direction giants of fear and hopelessness bore down on her.

She felt someone touch her arm. The reminder of her friend's presence loosened her tongue enough to let a few words slip out.

"We're not sure yet," she replied quietly.

Mr. North's eyebrows bunched together. Anna stepped forward. "Emery and I talked last night and thought it best if I went with her if she decides to go. Will that be a problem?"

A dash of panic flickered across Mr. North's face before he could hide it. "No, it's no problem at all," he answered, shifting his feet.

Emery eyed him, his sudden nervousness setting off a tiny alarm in the back of her mind. Before she could dwell any further on it, he spoke again.

"If you decide to go, which I hope you do, you have my card with my number on it."

Her mind snagged on his words. "What do you mean you hope I'll go?"

"If I may," he began. "Your uncle must have wanted you to inherit his holdings, or he wouldn't have left them for you. If it were me, I would consider such a gift an honor and would seek to do my best to continue the legacy."

A sliver of panic shot through her.

As her thoughts tumbled over each other for supremacy, the pastor's message sliced through the noise.

The pastor had preached on Matthew chapter fourteen when Peter walked on water. He connected the passage to the storms in each person's life, emphasizing the importance of keeping your eyes on Jesus.

Emery had been trying to do so for a while, yet the empty feeling remained. After a while, she had gotten tired of praying and seeing no results, so she prayed less and less. Besides, her heart wasn't in it anymore. It seemed her parents had taken part of her with them.

She opened her eyes to find Mr. North and Anna staring at her. She looked from one to the other.

"Emery?"

She glanced at Anna, focusing on her friend's caring face.

"Remember Em, you're not alone in this."

Some of the heaviness lifted. Anna was right. She wasn't alone. She had her best friend with her.

You also have God.

Again, the thought came unbidden to her mind.

I'm trying God; I'm just so confused. There's so much I don't understand.

Turning to Mr. North, she tried to summon up an ounce of courage. Despite everything, underneath her uneasiness surrounding the situation, a small part of her wanted to know the connection between her long-lost uncle and her mother. And it appeared there was only one way to do so.

"Okay," she breathed out, surprising herself. "I'll go."

Anna smiled and gave her arm a reassuring squeeze.

"I'm glad to hear that," Mr. North replied. "If you don't mind, I can arrange for your travel and touch base with Mr. Finley at your uncle's estate."

Emery nodded weakly, too busy wondering if she had made a big mistake.

"Excellent," he answered. "I'm guessing I'll have everything arranged in about two days. Will that be sufficient?"

"Two days?" Emery squeaked, beginning to feel lightheaded. She felt a hand anchor her.

Summoning up the little strength she had left, she nodded.

Mr. North grew serious. "Are you also prepared to claim your inheritance as heir to the estate and business?"

Her pulse beat a rapid crescendo. Was she ready?

No, she thought, I'm not ready. But the answers to her questions lie somewhere in Rhode Island.

Opening her mouth, Emery tried to respond but only a squeak emerged. Clearing her throat, she tried again. "I…I'm not sure," she replied. "It's all so new right now."

Mr. North returned her gaze a while longer before nodding his head. "That's understandable," he said. "I'll leave you ladies to the rest of your afternoon while I begin making arrangements. I'll stop by your house when things are finalized with information regarding your travel plans." With that, he turned and walked away.

Two days.

Two days to gather her courage and brave the unknown, an unknown filled with a shaky past, an estate she had never seen, and a business she knew nothing about.

Chapter 3

Emery

Emery's hands were shaking as she went through the motions of packing for the upcoming trip. She had put off packing until she was ready, but two days had passed and now it was Tuesday morning, the morning Mr. North would arrive to take them to the airport.

As she folded her clothes and laid them flat in her suitcase, her mind replayed the past few days. Was it really only a matter of days since her world had been uprooted?

So much was about to change, and it didn't sit well with her. She felt the threads of her carefully woven life slipping through her fingers too fast for her to grasp ahold of. Every decision seemed like it was being made for her.

Her life had made a one eighty. Up was down and right was left. Now here she was, a girl from a simple town, getting ready to travel to a place she had never been to claim an inheritance she didn't know what to do with.

If she was honest, the idea of leaving the safe confines of her structured life bothered her more than becoming an heiress. She enjoyed her small-town life in Riverbend, nestled in the Indiana countryside.

Their town was secluded from the larger world, free from the confines and worries of big city life. Rarely did anything new or unexpected spring up. It was a quiet, safe place.

Now she was being forced to leave for an estate that would lack the comforts of home. *Home.* The word used to hold so much warmth. Now, it was merely a flicker of its former warmth without her parents to fill the house with love and laughter. Anna moving in had helped, but it wasn't the same.

Emery glanced around her room. Her eyes landed on a stack of books on the nightstand. An ache formed in her chest. She wished she could fit all her treasured books in her suitcase. She wondered if in a grand estate her uncle would have a large selection to choose from.

She swallowed past the lump forming in her throat, remembering how hard it had been to take a leave of absence from her job at the library yesterday. With no idea of what the future held, Mrs. Harris, her boss, was very understanding and agreed to give her some time. She had savored her last day there, running her hand up and down the rows of books, wishing she could stay.

Later in the day, she had decided to look up information about Mr. North and her uncle during her lunch break, hoping to find some answers. Using the library's computer, she searched for the firm on Mr. North's card, Beneath the Surface. The card had seemed legit, but it didn't hurt to be certain. After clicking on the link and exploring the website, everything seemed to be in order.

Feeling slightly better, she then typed in her uncle's name, Mr. James Adler. Her uncle's hotel chain, Adler's Hotels, popped up. The business seemed to be well established from previous predecessors.

Reading through articles and interviews pertaining to her uncle showed him to be a successful businessman with a charitable heart. All around, he sounded like a good guy, so why had he stopped contact with his family?

Knowing her lunch time was almost over, she searched for an article about his death. Steeling herself, she clicked the link, her eyes scouring the page.

The report stated he died due to a lingering sickness in his lungs. Someone had come forward with concerns of foul play, but it had been ruled out by police. Reading further, her eyes snagged on the last line.

"With no children to pass on his estate and holdings, his inheritance falls to his niece, Emery Wilson."

She sat back, her insides twisting into knots. Seeing it outlined in the article made it more real. She was an heiress.

Emery snapped back to the present. Brushing aside the questions fluttering through her mind, she returned to her packing. She tried to push down her rising emotions before they could break free.

As she picked up more clothes, she uncovered her Bible lying beneath the pile. She stilled when she saw it. Here she was bemoaning the fact of leaving everything familiar behind, of nothing being constant, and this one book stood as a stark reminder there was something constant. There was Someone she could lean on.

Emery stood still. Breathing in, she told herself she needed to trust God. She needed to have faith, yet a small part of her rebelled. A part of her wanted to stomp her foot like a child.

Things had been going well until the letter arrived. Now, her world was turned upside down again, and her old fears were waging war against new uncertainties.

TRUST ME.

The words stopped her mid-thought. She waited, but nothing else came. Sighing, she sat down on her bed, her fingers brushing her Bible.

Everything had seemed so much simpler when she was younger. She had grown up with child-like faith that everything would be okay because God was in control, so why didn't she have that same confidence now? Why was it harder to trust Him as an adult?

Her thoughts drifted back to Sunday's sermon about Peter walking on water, about trusting God with the storms of life. Why was it so hard to trust Him? She knew she needed to, but a part of her held back.

Emery hung her head. How was she going to make it all the way to Rhode Island? Tears began pooling in her eyes. She wished she were stronger and better at embracing change like Anna. Her friend rolled with whatever came, whereas she felt like she was the one being rolled. How did Anna do it? How did she remain put together?

A sob broke free as more tears leaked out. Emery covered her face with her hands, unable to hold it back any longer. It was like a pipe had suddenly burst, and once she started, she couldn't stop.

She felt the bed give as a weight settled beside her. A second later, her friend's arms encircled her in a comforting embrace. She leaned into it, letting its warmth chase away the darkness. When she felt calmer, she drew back.

"Are you okay?" Anna asked.

Emery nodded, wiping her cheeks.

Anna reached over and touched her arm. "I'm always here for you. Do you want to talk about it?"

Emery looked down, biting her lip. She didn't like acknowledging her weaknesses, even to her friend. She didn't want people to think less of her.

"Is it the trip?" Anna asked softly.

Emery bit the inside of her cheek. She should have known she couldn't keep anything from Anna. Slowly, she looked up, meeting her friend's gaze. The compassion she saw almost unraveled her thinly veiled control.

"I thought I could do this, but now…now…" She clenched her hand, willing the tears back. Taking a breath, she tried again. "I don't think I can do it. It's all happening so fast."

"I know it's a lot all at once, but you're not alone in it," Anna said.

Then why did it feel like she was? It was a nice thing to tell people, but it didn't change how she was feeling.

"Em, we can't always control what happens in life, but God promises not to leave us."

She looked at Anna, frustration, hurt, and confusion battling for supremacy. "Then why does it feel like He isn't here?" she answered, flinging her arms out. "Does He not see how hard this is for me?"

Anna remained silent at her outburst. Emery crossed her arms, knowing she should feel guilty for lashing out, but instead she felt justified. Was it so wrong to feel the way she did?

"You know," Anna began quietly, "my mom had a saying during tough times." She paused, reaching over to rest a hand on her shoulder. Emery had to fight the urge to pull away and run in the opposite direction. "She said you may not always like what happens in life, but God knows what He is doing. He sees the bigger picture."

Emery stared back at her friend. She could hear the truth in her words, but it was hard to accept them. "I know you're right," she replied, looking down at her lap. "But it doesn't make it any easier."

Anna squeezed her shoulder gently. "That's what friends are for, to help you through." She smiled. "I'll be right beside you every step of the way."

Despite herself, Emery felt her spirit lift. She may not like this turn of events, but at least her best friend was coming along for the ride.

Three hours later, Emery found herself standing on the front porch with Anna with her suitcase in hand waiting for Mr. North to pull up and take them to the airport. She clutched the suitcase's handle tightly.

It's going to be okay, she kept telling herself. *Anna will be with you.*

Glancing to her right, she saw her friend looking down the street, a smile lighting her face. She knew Anna couldn't wait to spread her wings and explore. She admired her friend's adventurous spirit. She sure could use some of it right now.

The screech of tires interrupted her thoughts. She turned in time to see Mr. North's black sedan pull-up along the street. A few seconds later, he stepped out and headed up the walk, drawing to a stop at the bottom step leading to their porch.

"Are you ladies ready?"

All Emery could manage was a small yes. As he took their luggage to the car, she felt Anna come alongside her and wrap an arm around her shoulders.

"It's going to be okay, Em," she said. "I'll be right beside you the whole way."

Emery looked at her friend and attempted a shaky smile.

"You might be surprised at how things turn out. It might be better than you even think."

She could only hope her friend's words came true. Threading her arm through hers, Anna pulled her to the car and towards the start of the next chapter in their story. If only she could look ahead and see how it would end.

After a two hour car ride, Emery found herself at the airport. She had never flown before, and her mind was quick to conjure all the possible scenarios that could go wrong. Anna had tried to console her by saying it would shorten their trip time, but the fact did little to comfort her. Being suspended thousands of feet in the air was enough to put her fragile nerves on edge, more so than normal anyway.

While she felt wound up tighter than a corkscrew, Anna bounced with barely contained energy. The sight made her momentarily forget her worries, bringing the hint of a smile to her lips.

Her friend had seemed to come alive the further they drove from their hometown. Emery knew Anna had longed to escape Riverbend for a while; she just hadn't imagined it would happen this way.

Anna walked back towards her, her smile in full bloom. "Isn't this the best?" she exclaimed, waving her arm towards the plane. "Not only do we get to fly, but we're flying in a private jet!"

Emery glanced at the plane. Mr. Finley, her uncle's business manager, had arranged a jet for them. Not for the first time, she wished she knew more about her uncle and what she was walking into.

After coming home from work on Monday, she had searched through her mother's things tucked away in a closet but hadn't come across anything related to her uncle. If they had corresponded somehow, it couldn't have been by email because her mother didn't own a computer and only had a flip phone. Texting was a possibility, but Emery was doubtful.

Her mother hadn't been very tech savvy, saying she had grown up just fine without the latest gadgets. As a result, Emery had grown up without much in the way of electronics, but she had been okay because she had her beloved books.

Her books had been her companions growing up. As an only child growing up in a small town, there had been no one to play with besides Anna. Emery was grateful for her friendship. Anna was the sister she never had, and she had been there for her through the ups and downs. Emery leaned heavily on their bond when her father suddenly disappeared one day.

She remembered the day vividly. She had gone into work like normal, unaware of how soon her life would change. Her father had taken time off work to go on a mini vacation to hike in the mountains of Colorado. When her mother hadn't heard from him in a few days, she grew concerned and tried contacting him and the place he was staying, but he hadn't checked in.

More days passed and their concern only grew. Emery feared the worst, but her mother tried to remain optimistic, saying no news was good news.

After a week, the police still hadn't turned anything up, so her mother decided to go and search for him herself. Emery had stayed with Anna, not wanting to be home alone. Anna did her best to keep Emery busy, but it was hard to distract herself.

Needing reassurance, she had checked in with her mother each night. For a few days everything was fine, but then one night she couldn't reach her. It kept going to voicemail. The more voice recordings she heard, the more her dread increased.

Anna and her parents helped Emery contact the police and update them on the latest development. The police made contacts throughout the area, both locally and in Colorado where her mother was last known to be, but nothing turned up.

Weeks stretched into months. Emery tried to brace herself for the inevitable, but nothing prepared her for the day the police showed up at Anna's door confirming her greatest fear – her parents were presumed dead.

After that, she wandered around in a fog. Nothing was the same again. Anna's family took her in, but she was so numb nothing mattered. The months after were a blur. It was like her mind had blocked it from her memory.

In time, she slowly came out of her shell, but she wasn't the same person. She had always been introverted, but now it was cemented in her. She didn't look for new friendships because that meant more heartbreak. Anna and her family were enough.

Her church family had been there for her too, but her attendance had taken a hit at the beginning of her parents' disappearance. She hadn't been able to bring herself to leave the house or do much of anything during that time.

Eventually, she had made her way back to church, and they had welcomed her with open arms as if she had never left. Their warm welcome helped thaw the edges of her heart, especially the parts that had grown distant towards God. Despite growing up in church, this had shaken her to the core.

She remembered feeling lost and confused, questioning why her parents were gone. Older ladies from church had come alongside her and tried to help her through it, praying for her and giving her verses and encouragement. After some time, she began reading her Bible again and praying some, but it wasn't the same. It was like she was a shadow of her former self.

Now, here she stood at an airport, waiting to board a plane and go to a place that would unearth all the painful memories she had tried to bury. She could feel her old fears and insecurities fighting their way to the surface.

"Em, they're ready for us."

Anna's voice broke through her walk down memory lane. Emery shook her head to clear it. Looking ahead, she saw Anna standing by Mr. North, waving her forward. Taking a deep breath, she walked towards the plane.

A few minutes later, she found herself seated beside her friend as the pilot prepared for takeoff. Mr. North sat a few feet ahead. Looking out the plane's small window made everything seem more real. Like it or not, she was going to Rhode Island.

Chapter 4

Anna

Anna Lawson could barely contain her excitement as the plane neared its destination. She was finally going on the adventure she had always craved! Pushing aside her satiny, auburn locks, she gazed out the side window.

Looking at the ground miles below, Anna pondered her life. It wasn't that she didn't like her small-town life and the community she grew up in, but she couldn't deny the yearning inside of her to break free and spread her wings.

She knew the trip, or in her eyes the adventure, had the possibility of risks, but the opportunity to see a new place lit a fire inside of her. For the past few years, she had dreamed of what lay beyond the cornfields that hedged in their modest town. Now, she finally had the opportunity to stretch her wings, and she couldn't wait to see where she landed.

As the pilot announced they would soon be starting their descent, Anna glanced to her right. She knew her friend didn't share the same excitement. In fact, she looked ready to bolt. Anna prayed Emery would be able to relax soon. She knew this trip wasn't easy for her.

Before long, the plane was safely on the ground. They had arrived!

Standing, she followed Emery down the aisle and took her first glimpse of Rhode Island as they stepped into the sunshine. Taking a few more steps, Anna breathed in the cool air, letting the light breeze lift her hair in its gentle grasp.

Surveying the scene before her, she noted the airport was similar to the one they had left, but knowing they were in a new state made it more exciting. She smiled, eager to start exploring.

"What do you think, Em?"

Her friend attempted a smile, but was unable to hide the slight quiver. She threaded her arm through Emery's. "It'll be okay. Think of it as a vacation."

"I'll try," Emery replied. "It's just a little overwhelming."

Anna gave her arm a reassuring squeeze. "We can take it as fast as you want," she said. "Whenever it gets to be too much, we'll take a break and enjoy the sights."

Emery gave her a small smile. "Thanks for always being there."

"Anytime," she answered.

When Mr. North said the car was loaded and ready, they headed his way. Anna continued to take in the sights, marveling at the hustling and bustling of people boarding and deboarding, planes taking off and landing. It was so different from the quiet pace of the streets back home. It was energizing! With one last look, she clamored in beside Emery.

As the car left Providence airport, she pressed her face up to the glass, wanting to soak everything in. She barely registered Mr. North saying they would arrive at the Adler Estate in Newport within the hour, her mind remained fixated on the scenery before her. It was so different from their town of Riverbend.

Gone were the fields that stretched for miles. In their place were towering buildings with smaller ones nestled about. Luscious trees were sprinkled here and there, showing off their glorious shades of fall.

But what caught and held her attention the most was the view of the waterfront. Having grown up in a landlocked state, Anna marveled at the sparkling blue water. What would it be like to grow up along the water, taking strolls in the cool of the day?

She hoped they would have time to try it during their stay here. She had never seen the ocean, or any large body of water, so this offered a window into a world unexplored.

As they continued along, every sight and person fascinated her. Anna wondered what the stories were behind the intricately styled buildings and the people who walked the paths. She did her best to read the names of any street or building they passed, trying to commit everything she could to memory.

Before she was ready, Mr. North announced they were entering Newport and would arrive shortly at the estate. As they drove, he provided a little history of the town and commented on popular tourist sights. Anna soaked it all in, wishing she could start exploring now.

A short time later, they turned off onto what she thought was another road, but as they rounded a corner, her jaw dropped. She heard Emery gasp beside her. It was no road, but instead a driveway. A driveway that led to nothing less than a palace. She knew it would be impressive, but she hadn't expected this.

When the car came to a stop, she didn't wait for someone to open the door. She stepped out, marveling at the wonder before her. The massive stone structure looked at least three stories high with a tower set at either end.

Columns stood straight and tall like sentries, guarding the entrance. Perfectly manicured bushes graced the walkway leading to the front steps, separating the spacious lawn from the architectural masterpiece before them.

The scene before her belonged on a postcard, and to think this was all Emery's! She turned to see what her friend thought and could see the same muted shock mirrored on her face. It was definitely a sight to behold.

After their bags were unloaded, Mr. North motioned them towards the entrance. Anna followed him with Emery close behind. She continued to gaze around in amazement. Everything was immaculate. She couldn't wait to see the inside and the rest of the grounds.

When they reached the front door, Mr. North rang the door-bell. Its lyrical melody echoing outward. A few seconds later, a man opened the door dressed in a finely tailored suit. Mr. North introduced them to the butler. He nodded in acknowledgment before stepping aside to let them enter.

As Anna crossed the threshold, it was as if she entered another world. The high ceilings had beautiful moldings matched perfectly by the artwork decorating the walls. Walking further in, a grand staircase led to the upper floors as the hallway branched off into different rooms.

It was like walking into a museum. Everything spoke of wealth, a mixture of old and new. It was practically begging to be explored, and Anna couldn't wait to get started!

Emery

Emery felt as if everything was happening in a blur. Anna wanted to start exploring right away. She was too numb to protest, so she let Anna pull her from one room to the next.

The whole time she couldn't wrap her mind around her new reality. It was a far cry from their humble dwelling back home. Even the fanciest of houses back home paled in comparison to the mansions here.

The rooms seemed to be endless in number. There was a library, music room, receiving rooms for guests, various sitting rooms, and an enormous kitchen and dining hall. Bedrooms and bathrooms lined the upper floors.

When they reached the master suite, her uncle's room, Emery couldn't bring herself to enter. She needed more time to process everything before trying to piece together the mystery of her past.

By the time they finished their exploration, it was approaching evening. They were served dinner in the dining hall and were seated at a table stretching the length of the room. Emery wondered why anyone would need a table that could seat fifty plus guests. Their meal had been simple, yet refined, fancier than anything she would have back home.

After dinner Anna wanted to see more of the estate, but Emery felt wiped out from the trip, both physically and emotionally. A maid showed them to their choice of rooms, and Anna ran back and forth between them, exclaiming at every little thing.

Eventually Anna chose a room, and Emery took the one next to her. She didn't want to be far from her friend in an unfamiliar place. Despite the lingering unknowns and unanswered questions, she found her eyes drifting closed within minutes of hitting the pillow.

The next day followed a similar pattern. She explored the grounds with Anna. The backyard, if it could even be called that, went as far as she could see.

Shrubbery of all shapes and sizes outlaid the yard, creating little walkways. Flowers and small trees added color and depth to the landscaping. The tree line beyond acted as a gate, fencing everything in. It truly was beautiful, especially with the changing of the seasons in full bloom.

Her uncle's business partner, Mr. Finley, arrived around noon. He was a middle-aged man already starting to bald. A neatly trimmed mustache graced his face beneath glasses that gave him a grandfather feel. His smile and laid-back manner quickly helped put Emery at ease. She could see how her uncle may have enjoyed working with him.

Mr. Finley joined them for lunch and offered to give a tour of the business. Even though she didn't have any inclination of keeping it, she felt she owed it to him to learn a little about it since he was still trying to adjust to her uncle's passing and running the business without him.

From the stories Mr. Finley shared, he had grown to respect her uncle over the years and considered him a close friend. His passing had come as a shock to him. He explained that her uncle had been in perfect health prior to the sickness that took him.

Emery could tell her uncle's death didn't sit well with him, but she knew from her research foul play had been ruled out. She listened as Mr. Finley explained that the person who had examined her uncle's body had been suspicious that something was off, but the investigation had reached a dead end.

Surely, the police would have done their due diligence, she thought.

Before she could ponder any more about it, the conversation changed course, so she let the matter drop.

Shortly after he left, Anna developed a small headache and went to her room to lay down. At first, Emery had tried to distract herself in one of the sitting rooms, but she was restless. Deciding it was pointless to try and force her mind to focus when it clearly had different ideas, she opted to explore the estate more on her own.

Before she knew it, she found herself on the upper floor. Her eyes were drawn to the master suite down the hall. She bit her lip. Should she? Was she ready? Would she ever be ready?

The questions floated through her mind, rooting her in place at the top of the staircase. Finally, unable to deny the pull, she hesitantly edged to the left. With each step, her heartbeat quickened. She wanted to command her feet to turn around, yet they kept marching onward.

Soon, Emery found herself staring at the door to the master suite. Reaching out, her hand shaking, she slowly turned the door's handle.

The room was cloaked in darkness and smelled as if it had been shut up for weeks. Flipping on the light, she blinked against the sudden brightness.

After her eyes adjusted, she tentatively walked further into the room, taking it all in. A large four poster bed laid claim to the center of the room with windows gracing the wall next to it. A desk sat off to the side with a dresser beside it.

Emery made her way to the desk, hoping it might contain some answers. The top of the desk was in disarray, as if someone had hastily searched through the papers resting on top.

Picking up the papers, she glanced through them. Most of them appeared to pertain to her uncle's business. Laying the papers back, she tried the drawers and found them locked. Glancing underneath the desk and around it, she couldn't find any sign of a key. She would have to investigate the desk more later.

Turning around, she walked towards the bed. A clock and Bible rested on the nightstand. Emery let her fingers lightly brush the cover. Seeing it brought to mind a description she had read in an article about her uncle's charitable traits and generosity to his local community. It made sense if he was a believer those values would seep into his business life as well as his personal life.

Emery wondered if her uncle had seen it coming. Had he sensed he wouldn't recover from his illness? Did he have regrets? Why hadn't he reached out to his family at the end?

Figuring she would likely never know the answer, she started to make her way back to the door when a sound made her pause.

Stepping back, she studied the floor. Nothing seemed out of the ordinary. She began walking forward and stopped when she heard it again. It was a dull, hollow sound. Kneeling down, she examined the floor closer. Again, nothing appeared off.

Trying to figure it out, Emery rapped her hand along the floor. When it echoed the hollow sound from earlier, she rapped her knuckles in a wider arch.

After this brief experiment, she concluded the hollow sound centered around one particular floorboard. Her hands flowed over it, trying to detect any differences. Just when she was about to admit defeat, her hand snagged on a nick.

Leaning closer, she saw it appeared someone had used a knife or some sharp object to create a nick in the floorboard. It was barely noticeable, blending it with the grain of wood.

Feeling on the brink of something, Emery took a deep breath as she maneuvered her fingers around the notch, trying to find an opening. She tugged and felt it give slightly. A sliver of excitement began pulsing through her as she gave another yank. A few tugs later the board lifted from the floor, revealing a hidden compartment below.

Slowly, she set the loose board off to the side and leaned over the opening. She couldn't see anything without a light. She wished she had brought her phone with her. Taking a minute to gather her courage, she gingerly lowered her arm into the opening, inching it deeper and deeper.

Feeling nothing, she moved her hand to the side and came in contact with something. Her breath caught, her heart racing. Running her hand over it, it felt hard, like a box or container of some kind. Lowering her other hand down, she pulled it up.

Scooting away from the opening, Emery glanced down at what she held. It was a rectangular tin box secured with a latch. The box looked like it had seen better days. Dents marked it and the color was faded.

For a while, she simply stared at it, trying to calm her breathing. What could this mean? Would she finally get some answers?

Taking a deep breath, she reached for the latch and unhooked it. Raising the lid, she braced herself for what it might hold. She gasped. It couldn't be. Afraid to break the illusion, her hand hovered shakily over the contents a second before taking hold of them.

Lifting it up to the light, tears sprang to her eyes when she saw it was real. She was looking at her mother's handwriting. Handwriting she hadn't seen in a long time. Wiping the tears away with her free hand, she stared at the bundle of letters before her. The top one was addressed to her uncle in her mother's handwriting.

So, her mother *had* kept in contact with her brother. Emery's mind swam with questions. Why had she kept it a secret? And why had her uncle hidden the letters? Her gaze returned to the stack in her hand. They were tied together with red string.

Should she open one now? As the question formed in her mind, her other hand was already fingering the string. Deciding it wouldn't hurt to take a quick peek, she pulled the string, undoing the knot.

As the string fell to the floor, she laid the stack in her lap. Lifting the top envelope, she saw the one beneath it was also addressed in her mother's hand. Were they all from her mother? If so, had her uncle ever written back?

Desperate for answers, Emery opened the letter on top, sliding it out of the envelope. Unfolding it, she felt tears prick her eyes again at the sight of her mother's familiar scrawl. Blinking to keep the tears at bay, she began reading.

DB,

A looks forward to seeing you. It's been too long since the last visit. You may expect to see him at the designated time and place. I pray his trip will be safe yet swift. Perhaps someday soon the whole family can be together again.

With love,

SA

The words blurred as the tears she could no longer hold back broke through. So many emotions coursed through her.

Why had her mother lied to her? Why couldn't the family be together? Was it dangerous? If so, what was so dangerous about her uncle being in the hotel business?

She felt more of her carefully constructed life crumbling around her. How much of her childhood was built on a lie? Why the secrecy? What more didn't she know?

Sniffing, she swallowed back the remaining tears. What was she supposed to do now? She looked down at the letters. She couldn't bring herself to read any more of them. She couldn't handle any more earth-shattering news.

Emery went to work putting the letters and string back into the tin box and securing the latch again. She returned the board to its place and stood with the box in hand, her knees creaking in protest at having sat for so long. Bending over to rub her knee, her nose brushed the box. As she drew her head back, a scent tickled her nostrils.

She paused, a memory trying to surface. She closed her eyes, concentrating on recalling where she might have smelled it before. Then it hit her – her father's jacket. When he returned home from a fishing trip once, a woodsy scent had lingered on his clothes. The same scent that encased the box in her hand. Her mind reeled. What did this mean?

Needing to get away from it all, Emery hurried from the room. Closing the door quickly behind her, she raced to her room on the other side of the estate. Once she was safely inside, she climbed onto her bed and curled up, clutching a pillow to her chest. Why was this happening? Why couldn't her life remain the same?

TRUST ME.

She leaned back against the bedframe. Trust? How could she trust God when He kept changing everything she held dear?

She curled her body around the pillow, feeling buried under the weight of unanswered questions. She clenched her eyes shut, wishing her world would right itself and things would return to normal.

Chapter 5

Emery

Thursday morning, the chauffeur drove her and Anna to her uncle's hotels to meet Mr. Finley. Stepping out of the car, Emery saw the string of hotels wasn't large compared to other chains, but they were well kept and offered a view of the nearby waterfront. She suspected the view of the water was part of the attraction. Anna had wanted to go down and see the water up close, but Mr. Finley was already walking toward them.

As he took them on a tour of Adler's Hotels, Emery did her best to listen as he explained the ins and outs of running a hotel. She didn't know how he kept it all straight. It seemed much more complicated than helping Mrs. Harris run the local library back home. She couldn't imagine trying to run the hotels herself.

When Mr. Finley was called away to attend to an issue, he encouraged them to explore on their own, saying they would meet up in an hour for lunch. He was hardly out of sight before Anna tugged her towards the door.

"Come on, Em," Anna said, excitement infusing her words. "This is our chance to see the waterfront!"

"Okay, okay," Emery chuckled as she had to jog a little to keep up. Blinking against the sun as they left the hotel lobby, she was relieved when Anna slowed her pace to a fast walk. "You sure are excited!" she commented as she walked alongside her friend.

Anna smiled. "I don't know what it is, but I feel more alive here. I want to see and do everything I can."

Emery kept her smile in place until Anna faced forward again. With no one watching, she let it slip a little. She was happy for her friend, but wished she felt as carefree. Looking out as the sun sparkled off the water, the scene before her appeared bright and full of promise. If only she could say the same about her world.

"Em, come on!"

Shaking loose from her thoughts, Emery jogged to where Anna was standing by the water. For now, she would push dismal things to the side and enjoy this time with her friend.

Before she knew it, an hour had passed, and they were due in for lunch with Mr. Finley. Walking alongside Anna, Emery realized she had actually enjoyed herself. For a brief time, she had laughed and talked with Anna as they strolled leisurely by the water and sat in the shade of a tree. For a moment, it was as if nothing life changing had happened.

Now though, as they entered through the hotels' looming wooden doors, her current reality once again began sinking in. By the time they joined Mr. Finley at a table in the dining room, her earlier pleasure had faded to a dull hum.

"What do you think of Adler's Hotels?" Mr. Finley asked as he placed his linen napkin across his lap.

Emery followed suit, giving herself more time to formulate an answer.

"It's beautiful," Anna gushed. "Especially the waterfront! I think I could stay there all day."

Mr. Finley gave a soft chuckle, its deep vibration soothing Emery's nerves. "It is nice, and a popular spot for visitors to relax."

Noticing him turn her way, Emery attempted a small smile. It must have done the trick because he continued.

"I'm glad you both have enjoyed it. Now, I don't mean to rush you, but after seeing the place for yourself, do you think you'll keep it or consider selling?"

Emery gulped, glancing at Anna. Her friend reached over and gave her hand a squeeze. Taking a deep breath, she faced Mr. Finley. "Honestly, I'm not sure." She swallowed. "I can't imagine running it myself."

"You wouldn't be by herself," Mr. Finley chimed in. "I would be willing to stay on as manager and would help you acclimate to the business."

"I appreciate the offer, I do, it's just…"

"It's a lot to take in," he replied.

Emery nodded.

Mr. Finley sat back, his face contemplative. Emery hoped he wasn't too upset. She just didn't see how she could run a hotel business. Glancing around, she took in the cream tablecloths and small flower vases centered on each table. The ruby red curtains framing the windows along the two walls facing the waterfront were tied back with a thick golden rope. The sunlight streaming in gave the room a warm glow, like sitting by the fire on a chilly night.

"If I may caution you in one area," said Mr. Finley. Emery blinked, drawing herself back to the conversation at hand. "If you decide to sell, be careful of which offers you entertain. I would be happy to assist you, if that's the route you decide to take."

"You would be okay if the hotels were sold?"

"I must admit, it would be sad to lose them, but the choice is ultimately yours. I understand you may wish to return to your life back home, but I hope you will consider what Rhode Island has to offer."

"I will think about it, but I don't want to give you false hope regarding the hotels."

Mr. Finley nodded. "I understand, I won't pressure you either way."

Emery studied him as the waiter set the food in front of them. He seemed genuinely sad at the prospect of selling the hotels. If only she could keep them, but it was too far-fetched to even consider.

No one talked much during the meal, except to comment on the food. Emery had to agree with Anna, the food was delicious. The meatloaf she ordered was tender and tickled her tongue with its light flavor. She had to admit, she might miss the food after going back home.

After lunch, they thanked Mr. Finley for the wonderful meal and tour. Emery promised to stop by the hotel on Monday to discuss options moving forward. By the time they arrived back at the estate, it was late afternoon. Emery decided to retire to the library, needing a touch of home.

Walking around, she took in the welcome sight of books tucked neatly into shelves. Choosing one at random, she settled herself into a nearby chair and began to read. She wasn't sure how much time had passed when the whimsical sound of the doorbell wafted through the library.

Marking her place with the ribbon bookmark, she uncurled from the armchair and walked out of the room. She stopped partway down the hall. She could hear the butler talking to someone. A short time later, she heard the front door close, its soft thud echoing down the hall.

With the coast clear, she continued forward until she reached the grand entryway. The wide-open ceiling towered above her as the butler approached with an envelope in hand. Her palms began to sweat. Surely this didn't bear any more life changing news.

"Good evening, Miss Wilson," the butler stated, dipping his head slightly. "A visitor stopped by to offer his condolences on Mr. Adler's passing and asked me to give you this."

Emery stared at the envelope in his outstretched hand for a moment before reaching for it. "Thank you," she whispered before turning and heading for the nearby sitting room. With each step her breathing grew louder in her ears. *It's fine*, she told herself. *Everything is going to be okay.*

Sitting on the tan colored loveseat, she took a deep breath. Slowly, she broke the seal and pulled out the paper. Unfolding it, she read the contents.

Miss Wilson,

I would like to take this opportunity to offer my condolences at the passing of your uncle. I have known James for many years. He will be sorely missed. When I heard James' niece was in town, I felt led to reach out on behalf of my friendship with your uncle. If you find yourself in need of help regarding your uncle's business, I would be happy to offer my assistance. It's the least I can do for an old friend.

Sincerely,

Russell Sterling

Emery picked up the card that had slid off when she opened the letter. It read Sterling Enterprises with a number underneath. She guessed he was in real estate based on the building outlines drawn around the name. Setting it aside, she reread the letter.

What should she do? She thought about waiting until Anna returned from her walk, but uncertainty ate at her. She still hadn't told her friend about the box of letters she found. She planned to tell Anna eventually, but part of her wanted to keep the piece of her mother she had discovered to herself. She wanted time to savor it before dissecting any hidden meaning. She wanted to hold onto the image she had of her mother for a little while longer.

Turning back to the letter at hand, she wondered if she should respond. She didn't know much about her uncle's business besides the crash course Mr. Finley gave her earlier today. Mr. Finley, that's it! She would contact him about what to do.

Reaching for her phone, she pulled it out of her pocket and searched for Mr. Finley's name in her contacts. Since he was the main point of contact for the business, she had thought it best to put his number in her phone.

Her anticipation grew as it rang. She didn't like making phone calls, but a text didn't seem right given the situation. She was about to hang up and try again later when a voice answered.

"Mr. Finley? This is Emery." She tried to ignore the quiver in her voice.

"Hello, Emery. It's good to hear from you. Is everything well?"

"Yes, I, uh, just wanted to ask your advice on something." Emery hid the side of her face with her free hand. She was blundering the call. He probably wondered what was wrong with her.

"Of course," he replied. "What can I help you with?"

Emery took a moment to calm herself before speaking. "I received a letter this evening from a business friend of my uncle's. He offered to help and included his business card. I wasn't sure if I needed to respond back."

"It's up to you," he answered. "I think it would be polite to respond when you are ready. May I ask who the letter is from?"

She glanced down at the letter. "It says Russell Sterling." She waited, but only silence greeted her. "Mr. Finley?"

"Miss Wilson."

Emery turned to see one of the staff standing at the room's opening. "I'm sorry to intrude miss, but supper will be ready soon."

"Thank you, I'll be there shortly." When the man left, she turned her attention back to her phone. She pulled it away. The call hadn't disconnected. She put it back up to her ear. "Mr. Finley?"

"I'm here." His voice sounded raspy, an edge to it she hadn't heard before. "Don't respond to the letter. I will stop by tomorrow evening and handle it."

Her palms grew sweaty again. "What is it? What's wrong?"

"I don't want to frighten you or go into detail over the phone. Just know I have reason not to trust Mr. Sterling. Please wait until I get there tomorrow, and I will explain everything."

Emery's heart seemed to skip a few beats. The air took on an ominous feel. This didn't sound good. What was she going to do?

The smell of dinner tickled her consciousness, derailing her downward thoughts. Dinner. She would tell Anna everything at dinner and see what she thought.

"Miss Wilson, you there?"

"Oh, yes, sorry," she replied. Her hand shook holding the phone. "I won't do anything until you get here tomorrow."

"Good," he said. "Now, I don't want you to worry. I merely want to inform you about what I know regarding Mr. Sterling and urge you to proceed with caution."

"Don't worry," she replied. "I won't contact him without talking to you first."

After bidding Mr. Finley a good evening, she hung up the phone and headed to the dining room, the letter and card clutched in her other hand. She hoped this would amount to nothing, but she couldn't deny the sense of gloom hanging in the air.

Chapter 6

Emery

*E*mery awoke the next morning to the call of birds. She lay still a little longer, simply soaking in the peace of the morning. She sighed, wishing she could stay in bed and not face the uncertainties of the day. Her stomach rumbled, appearing to have other ideas.

Sitting up, she tossed the covers aside and swung her legs over. Within minutes she was dressed and ready. As she made her way to the dining hall for breakfast, her mind drifted to the letter from Mr. Sterling. What made Mr. Finley distrust him? Was it something he had done, or simply two personalities not mixing well?

Taking a seat at the table, she waited for Anna to arrive. Last night Anna had told her there was nothing to worry about, saying Mr. Finley would handle it. She tried to embrace the same ease as Anna, but she was still on edge. She had the feeling it was going to be a long day.

When one of the staff members put her plate down in front of her, she noticed Anna still hadn't come. She turned to the young lady leaving. "Excuse me, do you know where Anna is?"

As she turned around, Emery studied her face. She appeared to be the same age as herself. She didn't remember seeing her in the kitchen before.

"Miss Lawson has come down with another headache and wished to stay in bed to try and sleep it off."

Another headache? What was causing them? Maybe she was getting sick.

"Thank you, I'll check in on her after I eat."

"No…I mean Miss Lawson asked not to be disturbed."

Emery watched as the girl wrung her hands before placing them quickly behind her back. She gazed into the girl's eyes, their light blue reminding her of a lake. Instead of reflecting sunlight though, fear shone through.

"Okay," she replied slowly. "I'll check in with her around lunch."

The girl's shoulders sagged in relief. "Very good, miss." She made to leave but stopped. "Is there anything else I may do for you?"

Emery shook her head. "No, I'll be fine."

The girl inclined her head and left. Emery watched her. Something wasn't right.

Scooting back her chair, Emery headed up the staircase to Anna's room. Reaching the door, she knocked. After a few seconds, she put her ear against the door's smooth wood but couldn't make out any sounds. Maybe Anna was asleep.

Stepping back, Emery wondered if she could call a doctor. It wasn't like Anna to stay in bed unless she was really sick. Recalling the words the girl had just told her, she decided to give Anna the time she requested. She would check back in before lunch.

Returning to the dining hall, she ate a few bites of her breakfast and then headed to one of the sitting rooms. Emery nestled into the chair closest to the window and watched as the birds flew back and forth. Maybe someday she would be free like them.

As if on cue, her mind drifted to the letters from the past few days. First was the one announcing she was an heiress, then there was the stack between her mother and uncle, and now one from Mr. Sterling. Were they all connected? If not, what did each one mean? But more importantly, why had her mother lied? Why the secrets?

She thought of the box of letters beneath her bed. Should she read more of them? She hadn't even told Anna about them yet.

She chickened out at dinner last night. Instead, her and Anna had discussed possible reasons why Mr. Finley didn't approve of Mr. Sterling. Maybe it was time to give the letters another glance.

Before she could talk herself out of it, Emery stood and headed toward her room. Along the way, the butler flagged her down. He handed her a note from Mr. Finley. She thanked him and waited until he left the hall before opening it.

Emery,

Something has come up at the hotel, and I can't leave. Could you meet me there instead this afternoon at 2:00?

Mr. Finley

Why hadn't he called to notify her? Maybe his phone was dead? Emery glanced at the clock. There was still plenty of time to read through her mother's letters before meeting Mr. Finley.

Her stomach began turning queasy at the thought of everything. She took a few deep breaths. Like it or not, she needed to know more about her past. And if learning more about the business and the letters were part of getting back to normal sooner and finding answers, then so be it.

Her mind made up, she went in search of the butler before she lost her nerve and asked him to let Mr. Finley know she would be there. One thing done, she headed to her room and closed the door. She leaned back against it, her earlier courage fleeing in lieu of her next task.

Forcing herself from the door, she walked to her bed and knelt beside it. The lush carpet cushioned her knees. Bending over, she pulled the tin box from underneath her bed and laid it on the floor in front of her. Closing her eyes, she willed herself to be brave.

Looking at the box once more, with one quick movement, she flipped the lid open and took out the letters. Untying the string, she pulled the second letter off the top of the pile. Taking a slow breath, she slipped it out of the envelope. Her mother's writing brought tears to her eyes again.

DB,

I pray you will be safe with your upcoming trip. A and I would like to join you, but we understand your reasoning for going alone. Please be careful and let us know when you have arrived safely.

With love,

SA

Emery tried to puzzle out her mother's letter. Was she speaking of her uncle going on vacation, or perhaps it was a business trip? They never mentioned going on a trip to her. She thought back to the last trip her parents went on together.

It was about a month before her father's hiking trip. Her mother had claimed someone at their accounting firm couldn't go on their anniversary trip out west and had offered their plane tickets to her. Her parents had decided to go, saying it could be in celebration of their anniversary that was in a few months.

Emery looked at the month written at the top of the letter – September. Her heart stilled. The same month her parents went on their trip out west. Her mind racing, she picked up the first letter she had read and looked for the date – October.

The same month her father went hiking. The same month her parents disappeared without a trace. And the last letter written from her mother.

Emery fell back, dropping the letters. What did all this mean? What were these trips her mother kept talking about? Desperate for answers, she pulled another letter from the stack. This one had June scrawled in the right corner.

DB,

A mentioned an upcoming fishing trip he is taking with you. He said the fish were known to bite there and were likely to get a good catch. I inquired about joining, but he said it was a guy trip. I'll be honest, I don't like this. Promise you will be careful and look after A for me.

With love,

SA

Her thoughts were churning so fast she couldn't keep up. She brought the letter up to her nose, the same woodsy scent from earlier encased it. The same scent on her father's jacket from his fishing trip he had taken that last June.

Emery stared at the letter, feeling as if her mother was talking in code but unable to string enough coherent thoughts together to crack it. One thing she did know. Her parents knew her uncle well and wrote to him regularly. She also had a sneaking suspicion her parents' trips were not what they had appeared to be.

※

A few hours later, Emery found herself sitting in the back seat as the chauffeur drove her to meet Mr. Finley. She had hoped Anna would be able to come with her, but she still had a bad headache. She had eaten lunch in her friend's room and visited some, but Anna had grown tired, so she left and spent the rest of her time losing herself in a book.

She pulled out her phone to check the time. As she went to put it back in her pocket, she paused. None of the scenery outside looked familiar. Had the chauffeur taken a wrong turn? She pressed closer to the window. They appeared to be on the outskirts of town. She gazed at the neighboring houses, growing in elegance and size the further they drove.

She was about to call out to the chauffeur when they pulled off the road and down a driveway. Maybe they were going to Mr. Finley's house instead? The car came to a stop before a looming mansion. It was nearly the size of her uncle's estate. Rather than the appearance of a palace, it resembled a stone fortress. Emery shivered. If this was Mr. Finley's house, it wasn't very inviting.

The chauffeur opened her door. Stepping out, she took in the perfectly manicured lawn. It didn't boast the number of shrubs or flowery plants like her uncle's, but instead had neat tidy rows of miniature trees lining the drive and walkway to the front door. There were two levels of steps leading to the door. Someone was standing on the platform between them. From a distance, he didn't appear familiar.

She turned to the chauffeur. "Is this Mr. Finley's house?"

Sensing movement, she looked to her right and saw a man moving toward her. The closer the man drew, the more apprehensive she grew. It wasn't Mr. Finley.

When the man was within fifty feet of her, she relaxed a fraction. It was Mr. North. She waited for him to draw closer before calling out a greeting. "I wasn't expecting to see you, Mr. North. Did Mr. Finley contact you about meeting here instead?"

Mr. North fidgeted with the collar around his neck. "Yes, the plans have changed slightly. If you would follow me, I'll show you inside where we can wait for him."

Taking one more glance behind her, Emery followed Mr. North to the mansion. As she climbed the numerous steps, questions began to surface. Why wouldn't Mr. Finley contact her himself? After all, he would have her number from when she called last night. She paused before the front entrance.

"Is something the matter?" Mr. North asked.

"Why didn't Mr. Finley contact me directly about the changes?"

"Well, I happened to stop by the hotel for lunch and struck up a conversation with him. I offered to relay the changes and contact your butler. Perhaps he forgot to inform you?"

"Perhaps," she murmured. "But he's always been good to inform me the other times."

"Maybe he was busy with something," Mr. North replied, opening the front door. "Either way, he must have received the message if the chauffer knew to bring you here."

Emery contemplated his words as she stared at the open door. The dim interior gave the appearance of a cave. She glanced at Mr. North. "Is this Mr. Finley's house?"

"Yes, and he should be here any minute." Once again, he motioned inside. She hesitated. "Miss Wilson, have I steered you wrong yet?"

No, she thought. *But why do I feel so uneasy?*

Biting her lip, she stepped inside. Mr. North followed close behind and shut the door. There must not be a butler to greet them.

"If you'll follow me."

Emery looked up to see Mr. North a few paces in front of her. She followed him as he headed towards a room down the hall off to the right. The mansion's interior lacked the warmth of her uncle's estate. She gripped her hands together as she entered a sitting room.

Gold embellishments decorated walls sporting ornate paintings. She wasn't sure what they were paintings of, all she saw were dots and streaks scattered throughout the canvas. Moving further into the room, she noticed a fireplace on the far wall and a cozy sitting area circling it. She stepped towards one of the chairs, running her hands across the plush plum cushion.

The sound of footsteps drew her attention back to the room's entrance. She gripped the chairback. It wasn't Mr. Finley.

"Hello, Miss Wilson," the gentleman stated. "How nice of you to drop by."

Emery swallowed. She took in the man's attire. He was dressed to impress in a smartly tailored navy suit. His full head of jet-black hair had a streak of gray, lending him the appearance of a skunk. Dark blue eyes studied her over a hawk-like nose.

"I am pleased you decided to stop after I left you the note yesterday. I truly do wish to help ensure your uncle's legacy continues."

His words jarred her free from her trance. "Note? The only note I received today was from Mr. Finley…" The rest of what she was going to say died off as her mind replayed his words, snagging on one word – yesterday.

"This isn't Mr. Finley's home is it?" she asked softly.

"I'm afraid not," the man replied.

Emery gulped and adjusted her grip on the chair. "Who are you?" she whispered.

The man gave a slight bow, sweeping his arm across his middle. "My name is Russell Sterling. Welcome to Sterling Manor."

Chapter 7

Emery

*E*mery felt numb. Her sense of dread returning in full force. She looked to her right and saw Mr. North's eyes trained on the floor. Her gaze swung back to Mr. Sterling.

"I'm sorry, but there seems to be a mistake. I need to get back to my uncle's estate." She took a step to the side, her legs shaking so bad she wondered if they would support her weight for long.

Keep it together, she told herself. *You need to get out of here.*

Mr. Sterling centered himself more fully by the room's entry. "Unfortunately, I don't think that's an option. It appears your ride is gone."

What?! She turned, making her way quickly to the window on her left. Her hands broke out in a sweat. He was right. There was no car in the drive. Slowly, she turned back around.

"Since you have no way home, why don't we retire to the dining room for a light snack," Mr. Sterling replied. "That will allow us some time to talk."

Emery looked at Mr. North, but again he averted his gaze. She took a breath, trying to dig up some courage. "Like I said earlier, I really do need to be getting back. I can call someone."

She reached into her pocket and froze. Where was her phone? Her hand scoured the empty place where it should have been. Her mind flashed back to the car when they pulled into the drive. She had started to put it away when she became distracted by her surroundings. She closed her eyes. It must have fallen out in the car.

"That won't be necessary," Mr. Sterling stated. "Our chat won't take long. You'll be on your way in no time."

Emery didn't like the sound of it, but she felt trapped. She didn't stand a chance against two of them. She would have to hope for an opening and be ready. Meanwhile, she needed to calm her nerves enough to remain alert. She couldn't fall apart yet.

With no other choice, Emery followed Mr. Sterling down the hall with Mr. North bringing up the rear. Upon entering the dining room, Mr. Sterling motioned her towards a chair and took the one opposite her. Mr. North remained standing by the doorway. A man brought in a plate of fruit and glasses of water. Once he left, Mr. Sterling leaned forward.

"I'll cut right to the chase," he began. "What are your thoughts regarding your uncle's business. If you are wanting to sell, I would be interested in buying it from you."

Emery looked at him in surprise. Was this all to ensure he put in the first offer, if she decided to sell?

"I'm afraid I can't give you an answer. I plan to discuss things with Mr. Finley before moving forward."

"I see," said Mr. Sterling, folding his hands in front of him. She couldn't quite gauge his reaction, but he didn't appear happy.

Unsure how to break the silence that had fallen on the room, Emery stared at the food left on her plate, wanting more than anything to leave. Just as the silence was starting to become overbearing, Mr. Sterling spoke.

"Sometime before your uncle's sickness, I had discussed a business proposition with him, but unfortunately we were unable to reach an agreement. Perhaps you and I can come to an agreement."

"What kind of agreement?" she asked.

"One that leaves me in charge of the business."

She gaped at him. Closing her mouth, she took a deep breath and tried again. "Like I mentioned earlier, I am not interested in selling at this time and would need to consult Mr. Finley in any business matters."

"Yes, I recall your earlier statement, but I think you should hear my proposition before dismissing it outright." Her uneasiness returned.

Clasping her hands together beneath the table, she looked at Mr. North but found him staring at the far wall. She turned back to Mr. Sterling. "What is your proposition?" She felt her insides tighten at the smile that crossed his face. There was nothing cheerful about it.

Mr. Sterling straightened in his chair before speaking. "My proposition is that you marry my son Everett, which would allow me access to your uncle's business."

Emery stared at him in shock, her brain scrambling to process his words. That was not what she was expecting him to say. He couldn't be serious, could he? Mr. Sterling seemed to take her silence as permission to continue.

"My reasoning is quite simple," he replied. "I want to become a giant in real estate and need your uncle's business to help me do that. I know Mr. Finley will suggest you don't sell to me, so the only way to obtain the business is to have you marry my son. I will then be able to run the business through him since it will become his business after marrying you."

Emery felt her pulse quicken. The whole idea was absurd, yet Mr. Sterling seemed eerily calm. Looking for a loophole in his thinking she asked, "Have you discussed this with your son?"

Mr. Sterling waved his hand as if dismissing the idea. "My son will do as I tell him." She felt her palms break out in sweat. This wasn't looking good.

She didn't like confrontation or telling people no, but this was one time she had to put her foot down. "I'm sorry Mr. Sterling, but I can't marry your son."

"Too bad," he said, shaking his head. "I thought you would want to help your friend. What's her name again…Anna?"

Emery's blood turned to ice. "What do you mean?"

Leaning forward, Mr. Sterling braced his arms on the table. "I hear your friend hasn't been feeling well. If I recall, your uncle's sickness started the same way."

Everything faded away as his words took root in her mind. Feeling lightheaded, she gripped the arms of her chair. It couldn't be true! It couldn't! She felt tears prick her eyes as she looked up.

"You," she choked out. "You had something to do with my uncle's death, didn't you?"

Mr. Sterling smiled as if pleased by her horror. "Yes, it was unfortunate though. Your uncle refused to hear reason and sell me his business, so I had to take matters into my own hands. I had someone slip small amounts of poison into his drink and slowly increase the dosage over time so as not to arouse suspicion." He paused, sighing.

"Unfortunately, whoever performed the autopsy discovered something of a suspicious nature, and I had to do some quick thinking to evade the police's investigation. Another suspicious death, especially so soon, wouldn't look good, but no one would question me obtaining James' business through a marriage. It would be expected of me to step in to help my son and daughter-in-law."

Emery felt a few tears slip out. How could someone be so cruel? Now she understood why Mr. Finley didn't trust him. He was a snake. Her skin crawled just being near him, but she couldn't leave until she learned more about Anna.

She replayed his words, trying to find a solution. Her mind latched onto his comment about having someone slip her uncle poison. The staff had been helping care for Anna. Had one of them been slipping her the same poison?

Emery tried to push the rising panic down. She couldn't lose it until she knew exactly what was going on. She turned to Mr.

Sterling. "Is that what's happening to my friend? Did you send someone to poison her?"

"I wanted to ensure your compliance," he replied. "But as for who did it, well, you'll have to ask Mr. North here."

A strangled cry escaped her lips. This couldn't be happening. But when she looked at Mr. North and saw his eyes riddled with guilt, she knew the nightmare was real.

Why God? she cried. *Why?*

"There, there my dear," said Mr. Sterling. "You have no need to fear for your friend's health, if you simply agree to marry my son. As soon as the marriage is finalized, your friend will perk right up."

It took all her strength not to crumble into a heap on the floor. She didn't understand what was going on or why it was happening. The only thing she knew was that her friend was sick and would continue to worsen if she didn't agree to his proposition. Unless...

Emery raised her head and looked Mr. Sterling in the eye. "If you will make my friend better, then I will sell my uncle's business to you."

Mr. Sterling interlocked his hands on the table. "That offer has already expired."

Emery's brow wrinkled. "What do you mean?"

"I can't trust you wouldn't stick the police on me as soon as the deal was done." He shook his head. "The offer has changed, and trust me," he paused. "You don't want it to change again."

Despite the fear coursing through her, she would do anything to protect her friend. Gathering her courage, Emery gave her answer. "I accept your offer."

"Excellent!" he exclaimed, rubbing his hands together. "I knew you would see reason."

The only thing she saw was a cold-hearted man who only cared about money. When she got back to her uncle's estate, she would sneak Anna out during the night and find a doctor. Perhaps she could hide her safely away until she sorted this mess out. Should she go to the police? After everything that's happened, she wasn't sure who she could trust.

The scraping of a chair drew Emery from her thoughts, and she saw Mr. Sterling had risen from the table. "I'll have someone prepare a room for you," he said.

"What?" she asked, startled.

"You didn't think I would let you return to your uncle's estate where you could alert others of our arrangement did you?" Feeling her last shred of hope shatter, she hung her head.

"Come now," said Mr. Sterling. "I think you'll find the accommodations here to your liking. And it won't be for long. My son is due back tomorrow. You can meet him then and get acquainted before the wedding next Saturday."

Emery's head jerked up.

"Don't worry my dear," Mr. Sterling replied as he began to exit the room. "The time will fly right by."

After his departure Emery debated making a run for it but seeing Mr. North squelched the idea. Folding her arms on the table, she rested her head on them, letting the tears flow. How was she going to get out of this?

Mr. North

Alex North continued to stare into the distance long after Emery had been escorted to her room. It felt like a cactus had taken root inside of him; no matter which way he turned he felt a stab of pain. Holding his head Alex tried to will the pain and guilt away, but the image of Emery's tearstained face and defeated posture haunted him.

He wasn't aware someone had entered the room until a thud sounded near him. Unfolding himself, Alex glanced up to see Russell had taken a seat across from him at the table. Unlike him, Russell seemed perfectly content. In fact, he was practically glowing. Feeling sick to his stomach, Alex turned away.

"I was wondering where you had gotten to," Russell said. "But I needn't have worried since it appears you haven't moved."

Russell's words barely registered. Alex heard a sigh across the table. "Alex, there's no reason for you to look like you've just been to a funeral. You did what needed to be done."

He turned his gaze back to Russell. "I didn't think things would end up like this. You assured me no one would get hurt."

Russell brought his hand up to cover his heart. "I am a man of my word. No one will be hurt as long as the girl adheres to my rules."

Alex wasn't sure whether to believe him or not. He knew Russell was a ruthless businessman, but nothing quite prepared him to witness it firsthand. "You never mentioned forcing Emery to enter a marriage."

"True," Russell replied, leaning back in his chair. "I said if she didn't agree to sell, I had a backup plan. I told you upfront no one would be hurt with either plan. And as you can see, no one will be. Once the girl marries my son at the end of next week, her friend will be well. Both will walk away with their health in tack."

Their health maybe, he thought, but not their hearts. And that part was all on him.

"Come now, Alex," said Russell, letting the chair fall back to the floor. "Don't turn green on me now. You've done your job; you delivered the girl to me. Besides, didn't you need the money?"

The reminder only made Alex feel worse. Yes, he had been desperate for extra money to help pay off his brother's gambling debt, but now he wished he had tried harder to get the money a different way. With his brother's looming deadline, he had felt backed against a wall and had been quick to agree.

After this disaster, he was beginning to think he should have listened better the times he had attended church. His mother would be rolling over in her grave if she knew. She had raised them in church, but it never stuck with him or his brother.

Once he left home, he hadn't darkened the door of a church until his mother's funeral. After that, he went occasionally mostly to keep up the appearance of a respectable man. Now here he was, sitting across the table from a heartless businessman while the lives of two women hung in the balance.

Russell continued talking. "Once the girl and my son tie the knot, you can wash your hands of the whole thing."

He said that as if it was that simple, but the look on Emery's face would stay with him long after this was over. If only he could turn back the clock. As if sensing his retreat, Russell learned forward, his face becoming a hardened mask.

"And don't get any ideas about crossing me," he spoke softly. "You know what could happen." With that he stood up and left the room.

Emery

Emery drew her knees closer to her chest as she curled into a tighter ball on the floor. As soon as the housekeeper had left, her legs lost their remaining strength. Her vision blurred as tears cascaded down.

She didn't understand why this was happening. All her life she had grown up going to church and had tried to live according to the Bible. Why was God taking everything away? First her parents and now this.

Wasn't it enough that her life had been upended a second time when Mr. North had shown up with the letter? Now her best friend was sick, poisoned, and the only way to fix it was to marry a total stranger. What if the son was just as cruel as his father?

Oh, why had she gotten into the car? She should have known not to venture out on her own. She should have listened to the uneasiness that had plagued her ever since Mr. Finley's note arrived changing their plans.

Her thoughts continued to tumble around until all she could do was cry, having lost the capability to string coherent words together.

It was then, grief stricken on the floor, that a voice penetrated the darkness. It wasn't audible, yet it was clear, parting the haze surrounding her mind.

TRUST ME.

Emery stilled.

TRUST ME.

She turned her face against the floor, wishing the voice would go away. She had prayed when her parents disappeared, and nothing happened. What was the use now? She didn't trust God to answer her prayers anymore, at least not the ones close to her heart.

TRUST IN THE LORD WITH ALL YOUR HEART.

The words echoed through her mind, matching a verse she knew well from Proverbs. Emery tried to slow her breathing.

How can I trust You not to let another bad thing happen?

Bracing her hands against the floor, Emery slowly pushed herself up. She wasn't sure how long she had been crouched on the floor. Lifting her head, she looked around. Darkness encased the room except for the nightlights framing either side of the bed.

Suddenly aware of how exhausted she was, Emery pushed herself to her feet and walked over to the bed. Sinking into the mattress, she leaned back against the pillows. As her eyes drifted closed, Emery thought of Anna. Somehow, she had to find a way out for both of them.

Chapter 8

Emery

Opening her eyes, Emery blinked as she took in her surroundings. Nothing looked familiar. Pushing herself to a sitting position, she let her gaze glide over the room. Slowly, it all came back.

The betrayal, hurt, confusion, and fear flowed through her as the memories resurfaced. Feeling her emotions build, she took a deep breath. She wouldn't panic. She couldn't. She needed to keep her wits about her to try and find a way out. She needed to check on Anna.

The thought of praying came to mind, but she dismissed it. She just couldn't right now. She knew prayer was powerful, but her feelings didn't match up.

Emery raised her head, trying to find a way to distract her mind. She didn't have to wait long for an answer. There was a knock at the door, and the housekeeper from earlier poked her head in.

"I see you're awake," she said as she walked into the room.

Emery saw she was carrying a breakfast tray. As she set the tray on the nightstand, Emery took in her graying hair pulled back neatly in a bun. She guessed her to be in her late forties. Emery wondered how she could work for someone like Mr. Sterling.

The housekeeper handed her a note. Emery stared at the note before looking back at the housekeeper. Her face was impassive, yet kindness lingered in her eyes. Perhaps she wasn't all bad. Reaching out, Emery took the note, weariness weighing her down.

Glancing up, she noticed the housekeeper had already left. She hadn't even heard her leave. Looking down at the note, Emery decided it would be best to rip the band-aid off and see what it said. Before she could change her mind, she opened the folded piece of paper.

Emery,

My son will be expecting you in the receiving room at 10:00 am. The housekeeper will escort you to and from the room. Your belongings will be delivered this morning, and a seamstress will arrive later this afternoon to take measurements before arranging a new wardrobe for you.

Emery let the note fall onto the floor. She didn't need a signature to know who the note was from. A small part of her rebelled at the authoritative missive, but a larger part of her feared for Anna.

Could she trust Mr. Sterling to keep his word? And if he did, what did the future hold for her? Was she going to remain a prisoner in this manor forever? Would she see Anna again?

As worry began to tighten its hold, a phrase poked through its constraints.

TRUST ME.

Emery's eyes drifted closed as the words played through her mind. Why did those words keep popping up?

She was a tangled mess on the inside with no idea how to untie the knot. She felt pulled every which way by the tiniest whim of emotion. Tears pressed against her eyes, pushing for their freedom. She squeezed her eyes shut tighter. Her hand clenched in a fist at her side.

I'm sorry God, I just can't.

Lifting her head, Emery brushed her eyes, wiping away the dampness before starting on her breakfast. She didn't want to take anything from Mr. Sterling, but her stomach rumbled its complaint.

Everett

Everett Sterling stared out the window, trying to reign in his wayward emotions. He had returned home from a business trip late last night with hopes of sleeping in, but instead found himself roped into his father's latest scheme.

He knew his father went to great lengths, sometimes even outside the law, to achieve what he wanted. Occasionally, his father requested his help to carry out a plan or go on a trip, but mostly he worked in his office at the family business. He preferred the quietness of his office, away from people and more importantly, away from his father.

He mauled over the little his father had told him. What was he thinking? Marriage? How desperate was he to obtain Mr. Adler's business? Surely there was another way rather than chaining himself to an unwanted wife. He had always followed his father's lead, done his bidding. But this was one time he was tempted to refuse.

He knew to do so was risky, but perhaps if he offered a solution his father would be willing to listen. For now, he would have to meet his supposed bride. As if he conjured her, Everett heard the soft pads of footsteps. Slowly, he turned from the window, dropping his mask of indifference in place.

Emery

Emery steeled herself as she rounded the corner. Her gaze fell upon a young man probably not much older than her twenty-three years. The sun shining through the window reflected off of his dark brown hair. He had an athletic build and stood tall and straight, his face unreadable.

As she drew near, she noticed his eyes were a deep blue, but cold like ice. He seemed to resemble a statue more than a man, hard and immovable. She stopped a few feet away and stared back, unsure what to say or do. She looked to the housekeeper for guidance but found her stationed by the entrance.

Turning back, she found him studying her. Emery bit the inside of her lip. She wasn't good at starting conversations even under normal circumstances. They stood there for some time, until he finally broke the silence.

"So, you're the one," he said. "Emery, is it?"

Not sure how to interpret his tone, Emery simply nodded.

Everett

Everett continued to stare at her. She wasn't what he was expecting. She was shorter than average, only coming to his shoulders, and her chestnut-colored hair was pulled back in a low bun. Her attire didn't lend the air of someone who came from wealth, which surprised him since her uncle was a man of means.

Perhaps she had been just as surprised as everyone else by the turn of events. It was certainly a shock for the community to discover Mr. Adler had a niece. Why had he kept her a secret?

Drawing himself from his thoughts, he noticed her eyes seemed to be searching his face for answers. Not sure what answers she was seeking, he figured it would be best to learn more about her. He needed as much information as possible if he was going to persuade his father to go with another idea.

"Why don't we sit down," he said, motioning toward the chairs. She looked to the chairs then back at him before walking over to one.

Taking the seat on the other side of the coffee table, Everett pondered where to start. Where *did* one start in a situation like this? He supposed he should start with what had brought them here.

He shifted slightly to face her. "Why didn't you want to sell your uncle's business to my father?"

A mix of emotions crossed Emery's face before she spoke. "I had my reasons, but none of it matters now." She paused before continuing. "I eventually did offer to sell, but your father refused."

Interesting, he thought. He sat back, studying her. She gave no signs of lying, but her story didn't match up with what his father had told him. His father said she had refused to sell and as a result, he had to help her see reason.

"So, why did you come here if your original intention was not to sell?"

She straightened in her chair as fire infused her voice. "I was tricked into coming by my chauffer and Mr. North."

"You didn't come in response to my father's note?"

"No," she answered adamantly. "I was supposed to meet with Mr. Finley but instead wound up here." Her voice lost its edge as her gaze dropped to her lap. "Now I'm a prisoner." The last part was uttered so softly he almost missed it.

Everett rubbed his hand across his chin as he gazed at the woman before him. She was nothing like he expected, and he was starting to think he might have an ally in his search for a way out of his father's scheme. But first, he needed to gather all the facts he could.

Emery

The reminder of her position as a prisoner was like getting hit with a sledgehammer all over again. She tried to regain her earlier anger and push aside the despair. She had to keep trying to find a way out.

The sound of a throat clearing brought her back to the present. She looked up and saw Everett staring at her intently.

"What would happen if you didn't accept the marriage?"

Was it really possible he didn't know? From his earlier questions, she had begun to suspect he wasn't in on his father's trickery. If so, what had his father told him?

Realizing she hadn't answered yet, Emery quickly shook away her wonderings before speaking. "He said if I cared about my friend's health I would agree."

At her statement his eyes seemed to bore into hers with even more intensity.

"What do you mean?"

Emery looked away as she retold the story. "He alluded to my uncle's sickness starting the same as my friend's." Her voice softened. "It was then I realized he was the one behind my uncle's death and now possibly my friend's."

Emery felt a few tears leak out. Wiping them away, she continued as she gazed outside the window. "I would do anything to protect my friend, so I agreed to the marriage. It was later I found out I wouldn't be allowed to leave until the wedding at the end of next week."

Everett

Hearing her story cut a chord in him. He had always prided himself on remaining emotionally unattached. It was necessary in his line of work, especially the way his father conducted business.

He knew his father could be a hard man and wasn't above using underhanded means to get what he wanted, but seeing Emery's pain affected him in a way he couldn't explain.

No, he told himself, *I can't let myself grow soft.*

His father had taught him people didn't grow in this industry by being pushovers. Hardening himself, he straightened in his chair, focusing on the matter at hand. "Well, at least now we can take the necessary steps in moving forward."

Her head whipped around. "What do you mean?"

Keeping his face neutral, he replied, "I don't want this marriage any more than you, so we have a week to find a way out."

"Are you serious?" she said, disbelief coating her voice. "You will go against your father's wishes?" She hesitated. "He seemed sure you would go along with it."

I'm sure he did, he thought to himself. He had never given his father any reason to believe otherwise over the years. But this was one time he couldn't sit idly by, not when the consequences could last a lifetime.

He looked Emery in the eyes. "I'm certain. We can meet again tomorrow to discuss things further. For now, I have other things I need to look into."

He watched as Emery took his cue and left the room, the housekeeper following close behind. He had forgotten she was there. Unsure whether the housekeeper would relay their conversation to his father, he quickly left the sitting room and headed to the library. He needed to hurry while at the same time being cautious. Even without the housekeeper, his father had a knack for knowing people's comings and goings.

Emery

Emery barely registered the door closing before collapsing on the bed. Her body was tired from the emotional morning. Despite the glimmer of hope after talking with Everett, she still couldn't shake the question of why. Why was God allowing this to happen? Wouldn't it be simpler to just make the problem go away?

She thought back to when this all started. If she had known from the beginning what would happen, she would have agreed to sell. But Mr. Finley's ominous remarks concerning Mr. Sterling had given her pause, and now she was stuck in a seemingly impossible situation.

Emery knew God could work all things for her good, but she didn't see how any good could come out of this. What was she going to do? Hopelessness began wrapping its murky tentacles around her. She buried her face in her pillow wishing everything would return back to normal.

Emery wasn't sure how long she had lain there when a knock sounded at the door. She pushed herself up. Looking at the clock, she saw it was a little after eleven. Perhaps it was the housekeeper with lunch.

Swinging her legs over, she stood and walked to the door. She opened it to find Mr. North on the other side holding her suitcase. Could this day get any worse? She was tempted to slam the door in his face but decided against it.

"I have your things from your uncle's estate," he replied quietly.

Emery stared back before stepping aside to let him in. He walked just inside the room and set the suitcase down. When he turned to her, she saw remorse in his eyes. Did he feel bad about what he did or that he got caught? Needing to know, she spoke up. "Why did you do it?"

Mr. North remained silent. Just when it seemed he wasn't going to answer, he spoke. "I needed money to help get my brother out of trouble. I realize now I should have found a different way to get the money. When I took the job, I didn't know this would happen. Please believe me," he begged, his eyes beseeching her to do so.

Sorry or not, the facts remained the same. "But you still followed through with it," she answered. "Was any part of the story you told us true?"

Again, Mr. North waited before responding, as if gathering his thoughts. "No," he said. "I work under Mr. Sterling's employ and sometimes he sends me on special jobs."

"So, you're not a private investigator?" she asked, crossing her arms. "Did you ever talk to my uncle? Where did you get the letter you gave me?"

"No, I'm not. It's simply a cover I use when Mr. Sterling sends me on trips." He paused before continuing.

"I knew of your uncle, but never talked to him. When Mr. Sterling approached me, he already had the letter in his possession. My guess is he used blackmail or threats to obtain the information from your uncle's executor." His eyes seemed to be pleading with her, but for what she didn't know.

"Was your 'special job' to get me to come so Mr. Sterling could either force me to sell or marry me off to his son?" Emery asked.

"I was to bring you, but I didn't know about his plan to have you marry his son. He told me if you didn't sell, he had a backup plan, but assured me no one would get hurt."

Her eyes flashed with anger, her voice raising a notch. "You still believed him after he ordered Anna to be poisoned? Shouldn't that have clued you in that something was wrong?"

Mr. North closed his eyes. "If I could go back and change things, believe me I would." Opening his eyes, he continued. "Mr. Sterling didn't anticipate you bringing someone along, so when he found out, he devised a plan to get her out of the way until he had control of your uncle's business. He assured me the poison would be given in small amounts to make your friend unwell but not kill her."

If anything, hearing him admit his part in poisoning Anna only fueled the fire within her. "How did you do it?" she asked, heat shooting from her eyes.

He spoke slowly. "I gave it to one of the staff to slip into her drink. I didn't open the note, but I know she was given strict instructions of how much to give and how often."

Some of her anger dissipated. Her uncle's staff, who had been so kind to them since arriving, had turned on them. Could anyone be trusted? Deflated, she sagged against the wall.

"Miss Wilson, I'm truly sorry for my part in this," he said. "If I could do anything to help you or your friend I would."

She straightened from the wall, hope beginning to blossom. "Maybe you can," she answered. "You can ensure Anna doesn't drink any more of the poison."

Mr. North shook his head, his voice laced with sadness. "I wish I could, but Mr. Sterling is not a man to be crossed. My brother could be harmed if I cross him, and I'm sure the staff member slipping her the poison would face repercussions as well."

"But if you don't do it, who will?" Emery cried.

"I don't know," he said, shuffling towards the door. "I must be going soon, or Mr. Sterling will be wondering what is keeping me."

Emery watched the door quietly close behind him. Her emotions tumbled over each other. Needing a distraction, she marched to her suitcase and began unpacking.

Halfway through, her eyes fell on her Bible. Mr. North must have stuck it in with her clothes. Slowly, she grasped hold of it, taking it from her suitcase and laying it on her lap. She stared at it, knowing she should open it, but not wanting to.

She knew if she did, she would read stories of how God worked miracles in other people's lives, yet her life remained in shambles. If He could raise the dead, why wouldn't He help her? If He could heal the leper, why wouldn't He heal Anna?

With no answers forthcoming, she put her Bible on the night-stand. Maybe one day she would read it again, but for now she wasn't ready. Turning back, she returned to the task of unpacking her clothes.

Chapter 9

Everett

Everett straightened his suit before entering the dining room. His father liked to dress to impress no matter the occasion, and he wanted to do whatever he could in an effort to get his father to be receptive in forgoing the marriage.

When he walked in, his father looked up from his position at the head of the table and smiled. "Hello son, come join me."

Everett took the seat to the right of his father as he motioned the staff to add another plate setting. "Tell me," his father began, "How did your meeting with Emery go?"

He nodded his thanks as a plate was placed in front of him, buying time to form a response. "It was enlightening to say the least," he said. "She didn't seem keen on the arrangement."

His father chuckled. "Yes, it is a rather unconventional agreement, but one that will serve everyone well."

"How so?" he asked. As far as he could tell, it would only serve his father well.

"We acquire James Adler's business of course!" his father exclaimed. "This is what we need to get to the top in this industry. James' business is sitting on prime real estate, land that can be used to build grand condos near the waterfront. It will be a nice get for us."

"I agree," said Everett. "But is marriage truly the only way to achieve this? You haven't had a plan like this before."

His father grew more serious, folding his hands on the table in front of him. "It is unusual, but it is the only option. After I realized James wouldn't sell, I put a plan in motion to help change his mind."

"With poison," Everett stated.

"It is an effective method for getting one's way," his father replied. "But it failed in regard to James."

"What do you mean? He's dead, isn't he?"

Sighing, his father leaned back in his chair. "True, he's dead, but that could have been avoided had he changed his mind about selling. I paid him a visit when he was sick in bed and offered to stop it from worsening if he would agree to sell to me. He refused. When I saw he wasn't going to change his mind, I figured he was a liability and had him finished off."

His father paused as more staff entered, giving Everett time to consider the casual way his father discussed James' death, as if it was of little consequence.

He was no saint himself and was used to his father's methods of persuasion, but his father's look on human life was not one he fully embraced. His father didn't see a use for someone if the person couldn't help him in some way.

Everett's thoughts turned back to the present as he heard his father continue.

"After James' death, I intended to buy his business but discovered from his executer that it wasn't for sale. At first the man wasn't open to expanding on why, but after some persuasion, he revealed a stipulation in regard to James' estate and holdings."

Everett could well imagine the kind of persuasion his father used to get the executor to hand over information. Taking another bite, he listened to the rest of what his father had to say.

"I discovered James left everything to his niece, including his business. I wasn't aware he had any family, so I had the person I paid off to slip the poison to James search the estate. This person discovered a picture of a young girl with the name Emery written on the back, matching the name of his niece in the executor's letter. I then hired someone to locate Emery and later sent Alex to bring her here."

His father paused to take a few bites of food before washing it down.

Everett took a moment to take a drink as well, giving him time to ponder everything his father had told him. None of it surprised him. His father was like a dog with a bone when it came to money, but it still wasn't clear to him why marriage was the only option.

As if his father heard the question running through his mind, he continued. "I planned to convince the girl to sell the same way but had to revise my plan after learning she was bringing a friend with her. I needed Emery alone where she couldn't be influenced by anyone, so I arranged for her friend to receive small doses of poison to ensure Emery's compliance."

His father took the last few bites of his food, sighed in contentment, and relaxed against his chair. Everett, on the other hand, pushed his plate aside, unable to finish. He waited for his father to continue, but he seemed to have said his peace.

"I still don't see why marriage is the only choice," he replied. His father turned towards him.

"It wasn't my first plan, but a necessary one. You see, it came out that James' death might not have been natural, and the police began investigating those who were last seen with James at the end. I was able to elude the questions asked of me, but it showed me I would need to be more creative and careful with how I handled getting Emery to sell."

Creative for whom? Everett wondered. He was the one getting married, not his father.

"It occurred to me," said his father, "that if Emery were to perish the same way it would lead to more questions. But it probably wouldn't be questioned if an unknown girl, Emery's friend, were to die from the same mysterious illness since few would be aware of her connection to James through Emery. Of course, though, she won't succumb to the illness if Emery follows through with the marriage."

Everett mauled over what he had learned, beginning to put the pieces together. "You figured no one would question you acquiring James' business if Emery married me since it would then become part of the family business."

His father beamed as if he had solved the puzzle of how to get richer, which in a twisted way wasn't too far from the truth.

"Exactly!" his father said. "Marriage will also ensure Emery and her friend won't tell others what happened because we'll be able to keep a close eye on them. Besides," his father continued, "who would believe these two women anyway, especially when her friend will be fully recovered, and Emery will have willingly signed the marriage license."

Willingly signed might be a stretch Everett thought. Emery had just as much say in this as he did. After hearing his father's reasoning, he realized it would be trickier than he first thought to find a way out. His father seemed set on this plan, and he had to admit it sounded logical enough to work.

But like his father had said earlier, Everett would just need to be more creative in finding a solution that didn't end with him waiting at the end of an aisle.

Emery

Emery sat down on the bed, exhausted. Who knew having your measurements taken and trying on dresses could be so taxing?

The seamstress had left a few articles of clothing until the new wardrobe could be completed. Most of what she left were dresses, not exactly her choice of clothing. She might wear a dress to church or on certain occasions, but all the time? Give her sweats any day of the week, and she would be fine.

Wondering whether she had time to rest before dinner, Emery glanced in the direction of the clock, her eyes landing on her Bible. Turning away, she told herself she was too tired to read it now. Pushing aside conviction before it could take root, she stood up and walked to the window, leaning her forehead against the cool glass.

Sighing, she closed her eyes. She felt lost, confused, hurt. She yearned for the peace and comfort she had heard preached her whole life at church. When she needed it most, it remained elusive.

She thought of the people at church who had gone through health battles or great loss, yet they still followed God wholeheartedly. They hadn't grown bitter or fearful. How did they do it? What was she missing?

There was a small part of her that felt the urge to pray, but she couldn't bring herself to form the words. What was the point? If God really cared, wouldn't He have stopped these things from happening?

Emery eased back from the glass and gazed out the window. The majesty of fall was in full bloom, filling the world with vibrancy, a stark contrast to the sorrow and hopelessness coloring her world.

The next morning, Emery awoke from a restless sleep. She had tossed and turned throughout the night, worried about Anna and frustrated at her situation. The thought to pray had crossed her mind whenever she awakened, but she had dismissed it. She knew she should pray, but her frustration prevented it. She didn't want to pray in the dark hours of the night. She wanted everything to go back to normal.

Needing to escape the confines of her thoughts, she began going through the motions of getting ready. After getting dressed, she started in on the breakfast that was delivered while she slept. She normally was up early, but since being locked in, she found herself sleeping later.

Taking a few bites of the oatmeal, Emery noticed another note tucked under the breakfast bowl. Wearily, she slid it out and opened it. It was from Everett asking to meet him at 10:00 in the same receiving room as yesterday.

What could they say that might convince his father not to go through with the marriage? Did Mr. Sterling even have a soft side they could appeal to? Noticing the time, she quickly finished her breakfast and prepared to meet Everett.

Walking into the receiving room twenty minutes later, she saw Everett standing by the same window as before. He turned at her entrance but remained silent. She stopped by the fireplace, deciding to wait until he made the first move. She didn't have to wait long.

"Would you like to take a walk around the grounds this morning?"

She looked up in surprise. She hadn't expected to be allowed to leave the house. Not wanting to waste an opportunity to stretch her legs more than the length of a room, she nodded. "Yes, I would like that."

Everett held his arm out, motioning her forward. She started forward slowly, not sure what direction she was supposed to go after exiting the room. As if sensing her uncertainty, Everett drew up beside her and led the way down a series of hallways and out the back door.

Feeling the sun hit her face and the coolness hanging in the autumn air, Emery let out a small sigh. She wasn't an outdoors person, but after nearly two days behind closed doors, the outside was a welcome reprieve. They started down the walk as the house-keeper trailed some distance behind.

Everett

Everett took a moment to enjoy the sunshine while observing Emery. She seemed to have relaxed some since coming outside.

"Have you given any more thought about our situation?"

He kept his eyes forward, giving a nonchalant appearance for any prying eyes as he steered them further from the manor.

Emery sighed. "Yes, but I haven't been able to come up with anything."

He nodded, not surprised. He hadn't had much success either. "It won't be easy," he cautioned, not wanting her to set her hopes too high. "My father is set on getting your uncle's business and feels this is the only way."

"What would get him to change his mind?" she asked.

Everett had wondered the same thing all morning. It was the million-dollar question.

"What does your father care about? Maybe we can find a trade of some kind."

He shook his head. "I'm afraid the only thing my father cares about is money. He sees your uncle's hotels as a stepping stone to greater wealth for Sterling Enterprises."

"There must be something," Emery exclaimed, frustration lacing her words.

"My father is a hard man," he replied, understanding her frustration. "Once he sets his mind on something, it's difficult to change it." He paused underneath the shade of a tree and checked on the housekeeper. She was keeping her distance, yet always remained in sight.

He lowered his voice. "I scoured some books in the library for any loopholes with a business transfer through marriage but didn't come across anything."

Emery glanced up at him, dismay etched across her face. "So, you're saying it's hopeless?"

"Not necessarily," he stated. "Just because a solution hasn't risen yet doesn't mean there's not one out there."

"You really think so?"

Everett shrugged. "The alternative is to give in, and I prefer to come out on top of a problem. I'll keep racking my brain and will get back to you if anything comes up."

He motioned back towards the manor. "We better get back before my father suspects anything."

He let Emery go a few paces ahead while he followed behind. As he looked at the beauty surrounding him, he wished he could find a solution. He may not like everything about his father, but there was one thing they had in common, the drive not to give up.

When Emery neared the housekeeper, she paused and looked back. Noticing she was waiting he quickened his pace until he drew up next to her. Together, they walked side by side back to the manor.

To the watching eye, they appeared to be a couple. But beneath the surface, they were bonded by a sense of purpose. One that was proving more elusive with each passing minute.

Chapter 10

Anna

Anna jerked awake from another fitful sleep. Trying to blink away the fevered dreams plaguing her, she looked around the room. Was it day or night? She had lost track of time, everything blended together in a blurry haze. Even sitting up in bed caused her weakened muscles to protest.

Leaning back against the pillows, Anna willed her body to cooperate. What was wrong with her? She remembered having headaches and being tired, but now she felt like a rag that had been wrung out and left in the sun to dry.

Where was Emery? She couldn't remember the last time she had seen her.

Anna tried calling out, but found her throat parched, unable to utter a sound. Swallowing a few times, she tried again with little success. Looking for a glass of water, she saw an empty cup on the nightstand. Before she had time to bemoan her parched state, she heard a knock at the door.

"I see you're awake, miss." A young girl entered the room. She stopped near the bed. "How are you feeling?"

Anna tried to respond but it came out more like a croak. The girl held out a cup. "Here, this should help."

Smiling her thanks, Anna took the cup and lifted it with shaking arms to her mouth. The wetness flowed down, refreshing her throat.

After a few more sips, she handed the cup back. The girl took a look in the cup before glancing back at her. "You still have some left. Don't you want to drink the rest?"

Anna shook her head. The girl held the cup out. "Why don't you try? It's just a few more sips."

Anna shook her head again. "Maybe later," she rasped.

The girl hesitated before retracting her arm and leaving the cup on the nightstand. "Do you need anything else?" she asked.

Anna tried to formulate a response, but her mind was starting to turn fuzzy. Closing her eyes in concentration, she replayed her thoughts from waking up until now. What was she wanting to know? Beginning to feel frustrated, she wished Emery was there to jog her memory.

That's it! She had wanted to know where Emery was.

Opening her eyes, Anna turned towards the girl, forcing herself to push through the rising fog. "There is something," she said, her voice coming out as a whisper. "Can you send Emery in please?"

The girl froze like a deer in headlights.

"What is it?" Anna asked. "Has something happened to Emery?"

The girl fled the room as if hounds were hot on her heels. Confused, Anna tried to push herself up, but her strength gave out. Feeling her eyes close against her will, she called out for Emery, her voice weak as the tiredness became too much to hold back.

Anna awoke still feeling groggy. She couldn't remember the last time she had slept so much. She couldn't remember much of anything lately. Struggling to push herself up, she noticed light streaking in through the windows.

She wished she could go outside and bask in the sunlight, but right now she barely had the strength to sit up. For a while she simply sat, letting the grogginess slowly release its hold on her mind.

By the time she heard a knock at the door, she felt more alert than she had in a long time. She turned her head as the same girl from earlier walked in. She laid a tray with a bowl and cup on her nightstand. Anna's stomach gurgled in response.

"How are you feeling today, miss?"

Anna smiled. "A little better."

Something odd flashed across the girl's eyes. Anna paused. What had caused such a reaction? She watched as the young girl busied herself with the tray, tiding things that were already straight. What could she say to help put her at ease?

"I'm sorry, but I can't recall your name," she said, hoping to break the awkward silence that had fallen in the room.

The girl turned, surprise lighting her features. "It's Ella," she replied softly, holding the cup out to her.

Anna held up her hand. "I'm not thirsty right now."

Ella began looking uneasy. After hesitating briefly, she returned the cup to the tray. "I'll be back to check on you soon," she stated, taking one last look at the cup before leaving the room.

Anna glanced at the cup. Was Ella simply shy, or was there something else? The growling in her stomach reminded her of a more pressing need at hand. Reaching for the bowl, she took a few bites, savoring the chicken noodle soup. It was just what she needed.

Growing tired after eating, she put the bowl on the tray and leaned back against the pillows. She hoped she would get her energy back soon. As her body relaxed, she tried to recall the past few days, but all she could remember was sleeping.

Her mind drifted to Emery. Where was she? It wasn't like Emery to stay away if she was sick. She debated whether to call out to Ella to inquire about Emery but decided against it. She would go see

Emery herself after she rested a little. Her eyes were growing too heavy to keep open.

Ella

Ella Carter waited an hour before checking on Anna again. Cracking the door open slowly, she peeked in to find Anna asleep. Good, she thought. She must have finally drunk the cup.

Relief flowing through her, she pushed the door open and walked quietly to the nightstand. When her eyes landed on the tray, fear wrapped its tendrils around her chest. The cup was still full.

Her heart racing, she glanced sideways and found Anna still sleeping. Should she wake her and make her drink it?

Indecision gripped her as she went back and forth in her mind on what to do. She finally decided to wait until Anna woke up. As long as she still drank it today, she would be in compliance with the orders she had been given.

Oh, how she wished she had the courage to say no the first time, but she couldn't risk it. If the rumor mill started again, few would likely hire her. She needed a job to survive.

Unwanted, the words from the missive replayed in her head. Closing her eyes, she willed them away, but knew it was pointless; they were engrained in her mind.

I have another job for you. You did so well with the last one, I know you can succeed again. Follow the directions listed below exactly. You know the consequences of failure.

It hadn't had a signature, but Ella knew who it was from. Her stomach curled at the thought of this newest assignment. It had been bad enough last time spying on her employer, but poison? She had wanted to refuse, but with this particular man, no wasn't an option.

Wiping away a stray tear, she opened her eyes and silently departed the room, wishing she could turn back time. If she could, she would fix the mistake that had altered her life and backed her up against a wall, leaving her no choice but to follow through with the command concerning Anna.

Everett

As dusk settled outside, Everett walked into his father's study. Opening the door, the room was encased in shadows. From the dark wood paneling on the walls to the deep-seated red area rug covering the middle of the floor, the room gave off an eerie feeling, as if it held dangerous secrets.

He stopped in front of his father's desk, waiting for him to look up from what he was working on. After a few more strokes, his father laid his pen down and straightened to look him in the eye.

"You called me, father."

"Yes," his father replied, clasping his hands in front of him. "A business matter has come up that I need you to attend to. You will need to leave tonight in order to make the flight on time."

Everett schooled his features to mask his inner thoughts. It was nearing time to call it a night, and his father suddenly felt the need to send him away? He was growing tired of being pushed by his father's every whim, but he knew not to voice any complaints.

"What is it I'll be doing?" he asked, focusing on the discussion at hand. He listened as his father outlined what would be required of him. It was simple and straightforward, yet he wished he didn't have to leave for three days to handle something a senior employee could do. He needed time to find a way out of the marriage agreement.

As if his father could see right through him, he spoke up. "I realize someone else could go, but I want to ensure it is handled properly. I can't afford any slip-ups with the upcoming wedding."

Everett wondered if his father had an ulterior motive behind choosing to send him. Popping in for a random inspection wasn't difficult to mishandle. His father liked to do surprise inspections on his various investments to verify they were working to their full potential. He liked to squeak out all the profit he could.

Could his father be trying to send him away on purpose? Did he suspect he was looking for a way out of the marriage? He decided he better tread carefully. Whether his father suspected something or not, he did not like to be double-crossed. Things would need to be handled delicately.

After reassuring his father he would see to the task, he left to begin packing. As he walked up the staircase, he told himself he would have to keep thinking of possible solutions on the plane ride. He figured money was the surest way of persuading his father to change his mind. But how could he do that and still acquire James Adler's business at the same time?

Emery could agree to sell the business and promise to remain silent about everything, but that wouldn't hold up with his father. His father didn't like to leave behind loose ends that could unravel later.

Everett sighed as he reached his bedroom door. When had his life become so complicated? Turning the handle, he hoped inspiration struck soon or his life was about to get even more interesting.

Emery

The glimmer of hope Emery had felt earlier talking to Everett faded. She had started to feel optimistic after discovering Everett wanted out of the marriage too, but now her hopes had been dashed all over again.

Heaving a sigh of frustration, she flopped back on the bed. There were only a few days until Saturday. She needed to find a way out quickly. Why wasn't God helping her? Didn't He care?

Staring up at the ceiling, her mind wandered. She thought of Anna, wondering how she was. Was she better or worse? Did Anna think she had deserted her? Her shoulders sagging into the mattress, she closed her eyes against the rising darkness.

The whole situation was madness. If this were one of her books, a hero would ride in and save the day, defeating the villain. But there was no hero in sight for her. The only person who had offered to help her had been sent away on a business trip by his father.

You still have God.

The thought rose up before she could squash it. It wasn't that she wanted to walk away from her faith; she was just confused and angry. Everything was unraveling around her, and she couldn't put it back together. She thought these times were when prayer was the fix, but nothing was happening. Tears welled behind her eyes.

God, why aren't You stepping in? You know how I feel, how lost I am. I can't find my way out. I need You, but You're silent.

A few tears leaked out. She turned on her side, curling her arms against her stomach. She wished for how things were. She had been in the valley so long, she feared she would never see the light of day again. Would she ever experience the mountaintop? Or was she supposed to simply trug along, a lone soldier in the night?

Chapter 11

Emery

The creak of a door woke Emery from her sleep. Blinking, she saw the housekeeper walk in and set down a breakfast tray. Pushing herself up, she glanced at the clock and saw she had slept late. Rubbing away the lingering holds of sleep she heard the housekeeper say something.

Letting her arms fall back to the bed, she looked at her. "I'm sorry, what did you say?"

"Would you like to go anywhere today, miss?" she asked.

Emery fought away the remaining grogginess as she pondered her question. At a loss for ideas, she turned to her. "Do you have any suggestions?"

A look of surprise crossed the housekeeper's face. Emery guessed the staff mostly received orders and were rarely asked for their opinions.

After a brief pause, she replied. "I could show you the music room or library."

At the mention of the library, Emery perked up. Books were just what she needed to distract her. "I would very much like to see the library."

The housekeeper nodded and said she would be back soon to escort her. Feeling a spark of energy return, Emery started in on her breakfast.

Two hours later, Emery found herself standing before the largest library she had ever seen. There were floor to ceiling bookshelves filled with all manner of books. She walked around, wonder filling her. How did one person own so many books? It surpassed the library at her uncle's estate.

Feeling encouraged that finally something good was surfacing, she slowly wandered up and down the rows, her fingers brushing the titles. Having lost track of how many aisles she had passed, she paused as a book caught her attention. It was pushed further back on the shelf than the others. She reached up to grasp the book, but it didn't budge.

That's odd, she thought to herself. Tugging it again yielded the same result. Reaching up with both hands, she yanked and felt it give a little. Another yank loosened it more right before the shelf swung inward on itself.

Unable to contain a small shriek, she jumped back and stared at the opening. What had just happened? She glanced around, but no one was in sight. Slowly, taking a deep breath, she stepped forward.

Placing her hand on the wall, she leaned in. Darkness cloaked much of the space, but from what she could see it appeared to be a room. Steeling herself, she took a tentative step over the threshold. A few more steps and she was fully in.

Just as her eyes began looking around the room, a scraping sound came from behind her. Turning, Emery saw the door closing. Rushing forward, she rammed against it as it clicked close. She stayed pressed up against the door, her breathing sounding loud in the room. *Don't panic*, she told herself. *Deep breaths.*

Feeling her breathing slow, Emery turned to survey the room. It was bathed in an eerie glow, lit by nightlights along the walls. The room wasn't overly large compared to others she had seen. A desk sat in a corner with cabinets above it. Various filing cabinets and bookshelves filled the remaining space, creating nooks and crannies for darkness to hide.

Willing her feet forward, she headed towards the desk. As she neared, her eyes were drawn to the cabinets. Learning closer to see what they contained, she spotted bottles of differing shapes and sizes. She bit her lip. Should she open one?

Deciding she might as well since she was here, she gathered her courage and opened the cabinet in front of her. Reaching in, she withdrew a bottle and nearly dropped it when she saw the image.

The light revealed a skull and crossbones.

Emery stared at the bottle in horror, her heartbeat kicking up a notch. Was this some of the poison Mr. Sterling used on people? Was it what was being used on Anna?

Not wanting to hold it longer than necessary, she returned the bottle. Glancing around the rest of the cabinet's contents, she saw more skull and crossbones. How much poison did he need? Feeling sick to her stomach, she closed the cabinet door and rocked back on her heels.

Weary of looking in the other cabinets, she decided to investigate the desk next, hoping its contents wouldn't be as horrifying. Taking a deep breath, she surveyed the desk before her. The top was clean; no paperwork cluttered it.

Reaching for a drawer, Emery found it locked. Trying the remaining drawers had the same outcome. Realizing nothing could be found there, she turned to the bookshelves and filing cabinets staggered throughout the room.

As she neared a bookshelf, a scraping sound made her freeze. She stayed rooted in place, trying to pinpoint the sound. A beam of light shining in parted the fear clouding her mind. Someone was coming in.

She looked back and forth. Panic rose to the surface. Spotting a nook close by, she darted between two filing cabinets. From her crouched position, she tried to slow her breathing, but it stopped altogether when someone entered her line of sight.

Mr. Sterling's form blocked the light filling the room as the door closed behind him. Emery felt her heart beat a rapid crescendo. She couldn't remember a time she felt so terrified. What would he do if he saw her?

Before she could formulate an answer, Mr. Sterling moved across the room towards the desk. Shrinking further into the darkness, she watched as he took a key from his pocket and unlocked a drawer. With his back to her, she didn't have a clear view. From the sounds of it though, he appeared to be shuffling papers.

Emery closed her eyes. *Please don't see me*, she thought.

A rustling caused her eyes to snap back open. She saw Mr. Sterling moving away from the desk towards a bookshelf. She could only see part of him now.

Her heart felt like it was going to leap out of her chest. Each sound sent a jolt of terror through her. How did he not hear her heart beating? It sounded like a team of racehorses galloping for the finishing line.

The shifting shadows revealed he was moving closer to her hiding place. Clutching her knees to her chest, Emery closed her eyes, using all her willpower to quiet her breathing. The shuffling paused. Too scared to look up, she kept her eyes shut, waiting for a hand to grab her.

After what felt like minutes, the shuffling continued and then lessened. Emery cracked her eyes open and saw Mr. Sterling remove his hand from a lever on the wall as the door swung outward to reveal the library. She held her breath until he stepped out and the door closed, encasing the room in gloomy darkness once again.

She rested her head against the filing cabinet, relief sapping her remaining strength. She remained sagged against the filing cabinet until her heartbeat slowed its rhythm.

Straightening, Emery pushed herself to her feet, staggering a little as she got her bearings. She wasn't sure how much time had passed but decided to wait a little longer to ensure Mr. Sterling wouldn't be in the library when she left.

The papers on the desk caught her eye. He hadn't returned them to the drawer.

Curiosity drove her onward. Keeping her eyes downward to avoid the cabinets full of poison, she gazed at the papers before her. The harsh lighting made it difficult to read them. Picking up the top page, Emery held it close to her face, a gasp escaping as she read the name, James Adler. Her uncle.

She continued reading, her eyes sweeping across the page. The further she read, the sicker she felt. Mr. Sterling had detailed her uncle's comings and goings and how he conducted his business, including his profits from previous years. It was as if he had been studying her uncle for a while.

Turning the page over, she froze at the heading. It read: Steps to acquire James Adler's business. Poison was written beside number three.

It had been hard to grasp hearing Mr. Sterling admit to killing her uncle, but to see how he had planned it out caused her stomach to turn over on itself. Who would be so twisted as to plot another person's demise?

Willing herself to keep reading, she returned to the page. There were hurried scratches at the bottom, as if it was written in haste. Squinting, she raised the paper closer. She read: Ran into issue. Business left to next of kin. Who?

Lowering the paper, Emery contemplated what she had read. It seemed Mr. Sterling hadn't known about her uncle's will. Based on his detailed notes, it was a little surprising. She could only imagine how angry it made him to be bested by another person. Why had her uncle kept knowledge of his family hidden? Was it to protect them from people like Mr. Sterling?

She looked at the paper again. So how did Mr. Sterling come to find out about her? She remembered Mr. North saying he assumed Mr. Sterling threatened her uncle's executor to hand over the information. Was that true, or was it something else?

The thought of Mr. Sterling watching her sent a shiver through her. Her next thought turned her insides to ice. What would he do if he knew she had seen this room?

This room held the evidence the police needed to solve her uncle's case. They already suspected foul play but had been unable to find any further leads. Looking around the room, Emery wondered how many other people had met an unfortunate end. Did these filing cabinets hold more information on people caught in Mr. Sterling's sinister web?

The realization that her uncle probably wasn't the first to reach this end was enough to make her lose her breakfast. She quickly returned the papers the way she had found them and hurried to the door.

Taking a breath, she reached up and grasped the handle she had seen Mr. Sterling use. Her palms sweating, she adjusted her grip and gave it a tug downward. A scraping sound followed.

She stood still, straining to hear any running feet or shouts of surprise. After a few minutes, she quickly stepped out and hid behind a nearby bookshelf. Seconds later the door closed. The sound seemed to echo through the library.

When she still heard nothing coming, Emery slid down to the floor, resting her head on her knees. She needed to pull herself together before heading back to her room. If she came across someone now, she wouldn't be able to hide what she had seen.

Anna

Anna awoke feeling the most rested she had in a long time. She wasn't at full strength yet, but her mind felt clear, no lingering fogginess. Noticing light streaming in, she gathered it was morning. She had slept long enough, time to get up.

Turning to the side, she saw a breakfast tray. Ella must have come in while she was asleep. Reaching for a piece of toast, she consumed it slowly, pondering what to do next.

She decided the first thing she would do was see Emery. It felt like it had been forever since she had seen or talked to her friend. Swallowing her last bite, Anna leaned over to grab the cup, but paused as her hand wrapped around the handle.

A memory of Ella's anxious face surfaced in her mind. She went to lift the cup but was stopped by a sudden feeling of uneasiness. It felt like a weight pressing down on her.

Uncertain about what was going on, she released the cup and leaned back against the pillows. The uneasiness lessened and soon disappeared. What was that all about? she wondered. Needing to see her friend now more than ever, she pulled back the covers and swung her legs over the edge.

Standing, she grasped the bedpost, dizziness overtaking her. She remained still until the spinning stopped, and then tried moving again at a more sedate pace as she went through the motions of getting ready.

Twenty minutes later she was knocking on Emery's door. As she waited, Anna felt tiredness lurking at the edge. Her head might be clearer today, but her body was definitely not running at full energy. She knocked again before trying to open the door, only to find it locked. *That's strange*, she thought. *Why would Emery lock her door?*

She called out to her, but no response. She tried a few more times with the same result. Was she asleep? But why would she be asleep at this hour? When she had left her room, the clock on the wall had read 10:45. She was so engrossed in thought she didn't hear someone come up behind her.

"Can I help you?"

Anna shot in the air, nearly jumping out of her skin. Her heart racing, she turned to see Ella. Resting her hand over her heart, she leaned back against the door. "You scared me half to death."

Ella's face paled. Realizing her joke may have been ill-timed considering how she had been bed-ridden, she quickly tried to smooth it over. "I'm okay, don't worry." She paused, but when Ella didn't offer a response, she continued. "Do you know where Emery is? I was looking for her, but found her door locked."

***

Ella

Anna's question was like a sucker punch to the stomach. Why had she let herself get entangled with all this? She should have known better than to agree to Mr. Sterling's demands the first time.

Mr. Sterling would not like to hear Anna was up and about looking for Emery. She had been given strict instructions Anna was to remain sick in bed until the wedding was over. Her body nearly broke out in a sweat at the thought of what the repercussions may be for failure.

Willing her face to relax, she looked at Anna. "Sorry," she said. "I was lost in thought. Why don't you take a short rest? You're looking a bit tired. We can see Emery later."

***

Anna

Anna studied Ella. Something wasn't quite right. The urgency to see Emery was stronger than ever, but she could feel her tiredness growing at a rapid pace. Maybe she should rest for a while before seeing Emery. Surely nothing too dire had happened. Maybe Emery had met with Mr. Finley about something.

"Alright," she replied. "I suppose I could use a quick nap."

A relieved smile broke across Ella's face. "Good," she responded. "Let me see you back to your room, and then I'll check on Emery for you."

She started back down the hall with Ella falling in behind her. With each step she felt her tiredness increasing. She wondered how long it would be until she was at full strength.

Arriving at her room, she thanked Ella before entering and closing the door behind her. She was only a few steps away when she heard a click, the sound instantly chasing part of the tiredness away.

Turning back to the door, Anna tried the handle and found it locked. What? Tugging a few more times didn't change anything. She started pounding on the door, calling out for Ella. When she didn't hear a response, panic started rising in her chest. Why would Ella lock the door? Was Emery locked in her room too?

Anna kept trying the door with no success. Sliding to the floor, she leaned her head against the door and tried to control her breathing.

<hr>

Ella

Ella stood silent at the other side of the door. Each thud and plea was like a knife into her heart. She wished she could help Anna and Emery get out of this mess, but she was too far in to climb her way out. Maybe she could simply keep Anna locked up and not feed her any more poison. Wanting to proceed with caution, she backed away and headed to her room, needing time to think things over.

Chapter 12

Emery

Emery felt like she jumped at every sound inside her room, thinking it was Mr. Sterling coming after her. When she had gathered her nerves in the library, she left her hiding place and ran into the housekeeper a few bookshelves over.

The housekeeper seemed frantic until her eyes lit on Emery, relief quickly filling her features. Emery could only imagine what might befall her if she lost her charge. Did Mr. Sterling use poison on his staff too? Not wanting to think about the possibility, she had dutifully followed the housekeeper back to her room where she had been served lunch shortly after.

Now she was pacing her room unable to sit still. What was she going to do? Someone was sure to notice her jumpiness. She stopped and took slow, deep breaths. Soon, her breathing slowed, but her mind was still racing.

Sitting on the edge of her bed, she held her head in both hands. She tried to will her thoughts to clear and forget what she had seen. Tears pricked the inside of her eyelids. It wasn't working.

Despair began creeping in as she let her arms fall. She gripped her hands together in her lap as the tears flowed more freely, a few drops hitting her hands. The tightness in her chest grew to the point of bursting. Fear and hopelessness coursed through her, filling her veins.

She clutched the neckline of her dress tightly, her body hunching over under the weight pressing down on her. A sob broke free as she slid to the floor, one arm holding her body upright from a kneeling position.

I'm so sorry God, she cried. *I'm sorry.* Sobs shook her body.

I don't know what to do. I can't see a way out. Please…please help me.

The tears continued to flow as she knelt silently on the floor. With each sob, it was as if part of her fell away. Would there be enough to put back together?

After a while, the river flowing down her cheeks dried up. She leaned back against the bed, the tightness easing some. Tiredness seeped into her bones.

Slowly, she reached to the side and pulled herself up onto the bed. Crawling to her pillow, she curled into a ball beneath the covers, clutching the blanket under her chin. She felt numb. Closing her eyes, she gave in to the tiredness lurking beneath the surface.

Ella

Ella tried to calm her nerves as she neared Anna's door, but she couldn't stop her hand from shaking as she inserted the key into the lock. Slipping the key back into her pocket, she eased the door open to find Anna sitting in bed.

She approached slowly, clutching the tray tightly in her hands. Her hands quivering, she set the tray on the nightstand, wondering what to say.

"Why did you lock me in?" Anna asked.

Ella kept her gaze fixated on the tray. "I can't say, miss," she whispered.

"You don't know or won't say?" questioned Anna.

She wished she could be anywhere but here having this conversation. What could she say without getting in trouble, or having Anna think she was a monster? While racking her brain for an answer, she heard movement.

Glancing to the side, she saw Anna had moved to the edge of the bed, attempting to stand. She started to panic. What if Anna made a run for it?

In an effort to divert Anna's attention, she gestured to the tray. "Why don't you have some food? It'll help give you strength."

Anna looked at the tray and then back at her, shaking her head. "Not now," she replied. "I would rather know what's going on. Is Emery locked up too?"

Ella froze.

"Never mind," Anna said. "I'll go see myself."

Seeing Anna stand and slowly make her way around the bed sent her into motion. Running to cut her off, she held her hands up, forcing Anna to stop. Her emotions felt ready to bubble over. "Please, you can't go," she cried.

Anna tilted her head, studying her. Straining to keep her tears in check, she tried again. "Everything will work out fine if you stay here." She stopped, realizing she may have said too much.

"Okay," Anna began. "I won't leave for now." Ella nearly sagged in relief. "If," Anna continued, "you tell me what's going on."

Ella's insides tightened. She wished she could tell her, but what would she think? Her gaze fell to the floor, boring into the lush carpet. Who was she kidding? No one would want to be around her after this stunt. Who would be friends with someone who poisoned another person?

She bit her lip. Maybe she should make a run for it. Anna could be free to recover and help her friend, giving her time to get far away from Mr. Sterling. Even as she thought it, the threat looming over her surfaced. Her shoulders drooped.

When she felt a hand on her arm, she nearly jumped out of her skin. She glanced up and found Anna's gentle gaze. "Please, I'm only trying to help my friend and figure out what's happening." Anna motioned towards the bed. "Why don't we sit and talk?"

At first Ella remained rooted in place, but part of her urged her forward. She let Anna guide her to the bed and took a seat on the edge. She sat stiffly, ready to flee at a moment's notice.

"How long have you worked here?"

Ella focused her attention on her hands. She supposed answering Anna's question was harmless enough. "A little over a year," she replied softly.

"Do you enjoy it?"

Hardly, she thought. She studied her fingernails. What answer could she give Anna? She couldn't very well tell her she had responded to a help wanted ad from Mr. Sterling, only to discover he was a vile man. But in need of money, she had accepted the position.

Her fingers curled inward. That decision had proven to be a grave mistake. After only a month in his employ, Mr. Sterling had sent her as a spy into Mr. Adler's household. The longer she worked under Mr. Adler, the more she realized he was nothing like her boss. That made it all the harder when she heard of Mr. Adler's passing.

Nothing was said, but she had the sneaking suspicion Mr. Sterling was responsible. Fear kept her quiet, not wanting to be next. She figured she would return to the Sterling Manor, but he had her stay on at the Adler Estate. She was relieved until a few months later when she had been given her new orders.

A hand touched her shoulder. Ella turned her head sideways, peaking up at Anna. Seeing Anna's concern nearly undid her. "Ella, what is it? What's troubling you?"

She looked back down at her lap. "Please," Anna said. "I want to help." Tears welled up at the thought of someone wanting to help. If Anna only knew who she was offering her help to, she would quickly change her mind.

"Why don't you tell me about yourself?" Anna said. "Do you have family nearby?"

Pushing her emotions down, she nodded. "My mother doesn't live too far from here."

"That's nice," Anna said. "It's good to have family close."

Ella wished she could share in the sentiment. She loved her mother, but they weren't what you would call close.

They had grown up scraping to make ends meet. Her mother had worked two jobs, so she rarely saw her. When she was little, various neighbor ladies babysat her. Once she was in third grade, she had stayed home alone after school until her mother got back from work.

Her mother would barely have energy to fix a small dinner, let alone have a conversation with her or read her a bedtime story. It was the same in the mornings. Her mother would have just enough time to make her breakfast and see her off on the bus before leaving for work.

Thinking back to that time made her loneliness more acute. Perhaps if she hadn't felt so lonely, she wouldn't have made her first mistake. Not wanting to dwell on her past, Ella turned to find Anna watching her. She remained silent, not knowing what else to say.

"Do you see your mother or your friends when you're off work?" Anna asked.

She stared into the distance. She had people who she thought had been friends at one time, but they had been wolves in sheep clothing. Remembering the hurt and betrayal felt as raw as it did then.

To her, friends were supposed to stick by your side through the ups and downs, but hers had turned against her. She still had her mother, but she had lost touch with her after high school.

A squeak from the mattress brought her back to the present. She shook her head. "No," she answered. "I don't see anyone when I'm off work."

"Do they come to see you?"

Ella shook her head, almost laughing at the thought of her friends showing up. They probably wouldn't even acknowledge her presence if they crossed paths on the street.

"Do you at least have days off to get out?" Anna questioned.

She could hear notes of concern in Anna's voice but didn't make eye contact. "No," she replied softly. "I don't go into town. Besides taking a little walk around the grounds, I stay inside." A hand touched her arm. Ella turned and found Anna's green eyes filled with compassion.

Anna

Anna's heart swelled when she looked at Ella. She saw someone in need of love. It was almost as if she had no one besides her mother, and she didn't seem overly close to her mother. She sensed there was more to Ella's story but didn't want to push her.

"You don't have to tell me anything you don't want to," she said. "Just know I'm here if you want to talk."

She couldn't quite decipher the look that entered Ella's eyes. She reached over and gave her arm a gentle squeeze. "I better let you get back to work," she replied, removing her hand. "We can talk more later tonight if you want."

Ella's light blue eyes pierced hers, as if searching for something. Finally, she gave a small nod.

"Good," Anna smiled. "I'll see you then, Ella."

She watched as Ella stood and slowly made her way to the door. Before she left, she turned back. Anna gave her another smile, hoping to encourage her that she was a safe person to confide in.

Ella turned and slipped through the door, a click following. The sound reminded her she hadn't found out why she was being locked in. As much as she wanted to find the answer and check on Emery, Ella consumed her thoughts. Something or someone had hurt her. She wanted to help her. Kneeling before the bed, she clasped her hands on the mattress.

Father, she prayed. *Please be with Ella. Something seems to be haunting her. Please help with what's bothering her and protect her. Help me to know what to say and how to show her Your love.*

She kept her head bowed for another minute before rising to sit on the bed and eat the food that had been brought to her. It had grown cold by now, but she didn't mind. As she ate, her mind continued to drift to Ella. What was her story?

Chapter 13

Emery

After her discovery in the library, Emery found she didn't mind staying holed up in her room. She still didn't feel like herself, but she felt better waking up the next morning. She started on her breakfast of eggs and toast, contemplating what to do.

Looking around the room for inspiration, her eyes alighted on her Bible. It seemed she was continually drawn to it. Should she crack it open and read it?

Despite her plea last night, she had yet to open her Bible. Her anger at God had dissipated some, but hopelessness and fear remained. Could she trust God to help her? She knew He could, but would He?

She sat on the bed, her fingers brushing the Bible's cover. She had opened it many times when in need of a verse or guidance, so why was she hesitating now? It wasn't like this was the first time she had felt scared. It seemed most of her life she was worried or afraid of something. But something had changed within her after she lost her parents. Would she ever get it back?

She thought of Anna. Would she ever see her friend again? She couldn't imagine losing Anna. She had been a part of her life for as long as she could remember.

So has Someone else.

The thought drew her eyes downward. The Bible beckoned her fingers to open it. It appeared her options were either dwell on her sad situation, worry about Anna, or read her Bible.

Moving her hand, she grasped the Bible more fully, lifting it onto her lap. She scooted back on her bed, settling against the pillows. She stared at her Bible before slowly opening it.

She turned to Psalms. It was one of her favorite books because there seemed to be a verse or chapter for almost any emotion she might be feeling. Her eyes fell on Psalm chapter three.

As she began to read, she felt her heart grow still. The words seemed to speak directly to her situation. Tears pricked her eyes as she read verse three. She began to whisper the words out loud to herself.

"But you, LORD, are a shield around me, my glory, the One who lifts my head high. I call out to the LORD, and he answers me from his holy mountain. I lie down and sleep; I wake again, because the LORD sustains me. I will not fear though tens of thousands assail me on every side. Arise, LORD! Deliver me, my God! Strike all my enemies on the jaw; break the teeth of the wicked. From the LORD comes deliverance. May your blessings be on your people."

Her tears ran more fully down her cheeks as she reread the psalm. Placing her hand over the words, Emery bowed her head.

How could I forget? I've been so upset and hurt. I haven't really reached out for help or try to see where You might be helping me.

Sniffling, she opened her eyes. They landed on what was written under the chapter's heading. It said David wrote this psalm when fleeing from his son Absalom.

She reflected on what she knew of David. This wasn't the first time he had been on the run for his life. The first time it was from King Saul, and now from his own flesh and blood. David was called a man after God's own heart, yet he experienced hardship and was pursued by enemies.

Her mind shifted to Jesus. He had lived a perfect life as the Son of God yet was punished for humanity's sins and nailed to a cross. He had endured hardships and people out to kill Him. Even His own disciple betrayed Him. Emery closed her eyes. If Jesus experienced hard times, why should she expect anything different?

God, I know life isn't perfect and sometimes You let us experience hardships. But how do we trust You when we don't know how You will answer? What if Your answer is no?

She closed her Bible when no answer came to light. She knew nothing was impossible with God, so why was she hesitant to trust Him?

Deep down though, she knew why.

If she was being completely honest with herself, she liked to be in control and know what was coming. That was part of the reason she glanced ahead when reading a book. If she knew what came next, she could relax and better enjoy the story.

She now found herself in a situation where she couldn't skip ahead to know how things would turn out. It would be easy to trust God if she knew everything would be okay. She could relax then. Could she trust God with the unknown, even if things didn't turn out the way she hoped?

The day inched by for Emery. When a knock sounded at the door, she opened it to find the housekeeper on the other side.

"I've finished my work early this evening and thought I would stop by and see if you would like to join me on a stroll?"

Hope stirred in her chest. She hadn't been outside since her walk with Everett. That could be just what she needed to distract herself from everything. "Yes, I would like that, thank you."

She followed the housekeeper out the door, and then out the back of the manor. As they stepped outside, Emery tilted her head back, basking in the glow of the fading sun. Breathing in, she let it out slowly. This was exactly what she needed, a breath of fresh air. Lifting her head up, she continued walking along the path with the housekeeper beside her.

They had chosen a different path than the one she had walked on with Everett. This one offered a view of the colorful tree line marking one end of the property. She smiled at the beauty of fall. It was one of her favorite seasons.

They had only traveled a short distance when a gasp beside her made her pause. Looking to the side, she saw the housekeeper bent over, clutching her knee.

"Are you okay?"

The housekeeper took a few quick breaths. "I'll be fine," she said. "I think I just tweaked my knee a little."

Despite her brave words, Emery could see she was in pain. She glanced around, but no one was around. As she went to turn back, a thought sprang to mind. She froze, wondering whether to act on it.

With her escort hurt, she might be able to make a run for it. She could be free. She could make it back to Anna before anyone was the wiser and get her the help she needed. The more she pondered it, the more her excitement grew. This could be the break she had been praying for.

A groan from behind her broke through her mirage, sending the image scattering.

She sighed as her hope of escape dissipated. She couldn't leave the housekeeper to face Mr. Sterling's wrath. She remembered the look of fear in her eyes when she had found her at the library. She couldn't put herself first knowing the housekeeper would face repercussions for her actions.

Having made her decision, Emery helped her up and back to the manor. She felt despair wanting to sink its claws in her again. Would she ever be free?

It felt as if God had dangled freedom in front of her only to snatch it back. She was trying to do better, but it was hard when her circumstances continued to remain bleak. So much was unknown lately. Was God really at work when nothing changed?

She wanted to feel whole again, for her life to go back to normal. Times like this made her miss her parents even more. She wanted to feel loved, safe.

She knew God could offer comfort through His written word, but the circumstances she found herself in kept pulling her back under. Just when she was reaching the surface, another wave would hit.

Ella

Ella thought of Anna's offer to talk as she prepared her dinner tray. Her concern had seemed genuine, but she was leery to trust so quickly again. She wasn't sure she could go through another betrayal.

As she made her way to Anna's room, she decided she would see how things went. If Anna still appeared interested in helping, maybe she would open up a little. She would just take it slow, no more rushing into things.

She gave a quick knock before turning the key in the lock. She opened the door to find Anna reading in bed. She was curious what she was reading. She hadn't noticed books lying around the past few days.

Anna closed the book as she set the tray down. Turning to face her, she could see it was a large book. Anna must have caught her looking because she motioned to the book.

"Do you have one?" she asked.

Confused, Ella shook her head. "No," she replied. "I don't have any books, but there is a library here if I want to read."

She had never been much of a reader, preferring to draw or make up stories in her head when she was younger. Reading hadn't come easy growing up, and her mother didn't have a lot of extra money for things like that. She had learned to entertain herself with the little they had around the house. Her attention turned back to Anna when she started talking again.

"I mean, do you have a Bible of your own?"

A Bible? She thought only church people had those, and she had never stepped foot inside a church before. Her mother had worked every day, even on the weekend, so church had never been an option growing up.

At times she had wondered what went on inside of one, but figured she was too insignificant to be noticed by God. She came from a small family, didn't have any special talents, and was part of the lower working class. Not exactly someone to be noticed by God.

She shook her head in response to Anna's question. "No," she said, "I don't have one."

"You can borrow mine if you would like," Anna offered, holding her Bible out.

She blinked, staring at her. She would share something with her, a girl she barely knew?

"You seem surprised," Anna replied.

"It's just….you don't know me," she said.

Anna's forehead wrinkled. "It's just that," Ella began. "I've heard Bibles are sacred books and only people who go to church have one. It seems odd that you would give up such a book to someone you hardly know."

Anna smiled. "The Bible is a special book since it's from God, but anyone can have one."

"What do you mean it's from God?" she asked. "Did God write it?" She hadn't heard that before.

Anna paused, considering her answer before speaking. "The best way to describe it is God inspired other people on what to write. It's His words but written by people."

Ella felt confused. Did God speak to people? She thought He was a high up deity that didn't interact much with people unless they were big Christians who did a lot of important things.

"Here, let me show you," Anna said.

She watched as Anna opened her Bible and shuffled through the pages. "Found it," Anna said, pointing to something on the page. Ella found herself leaning closer.

"It says in 2 Peter that 'prophecy never had its origin in the human will, but prophets, though human, spoke from God as they were carried along by the Holy Spirit.'"

Holy Spirit? What was that? She noticed Anna looking at her but wasn't sure how to respond.

"If you want, you can borrow it and look through it. I would be happy to answer any questions you have," Anna said.

She looked from Anna to the Bible then back to her. Did she really mean it? She would share with her and then talk to her about it?

Even when she had friends, they hadn't wanted to discuss things. They had preferred to talk about boys, fashion, or anything other than real-life discussions. The few times she had tried to talk about more serious topics, they had waved it off.

Her mind back in the present, she glanced at Anna. She seemed different from her old friends. She seemed real. Taking a breath, Ella decided to take a chance on her.

"Okay," she said before she could lose her nerve. "I can read some if you really don't mind sharing."

Anna smiled, handing her the Bible. Slowly, she reached out to take it.

"I've marked some of my favorite verses or passages," Anna said. "Feel free to read those if you want. The book of Psalms is also good. If you open to the middle, you'll most likely hit that book."

She had no idea what Psalms was but nodded in response. "Thank you," she whispered.

Anna smiled again. "No problem," she replied. "Why don't we talk about what you read tomorrow at breakfast or lunch? We could spend these times together learning more about God and each other."

Ella felt her heart speed up at the possibility. She still wasn't sure God would notice a girl like her, but the thought of having regular talks with someone, a potential friend even, caused a sliver of hope to take root inside of her.

Despite everything, she couldn't keep a small smile from escaping. "I'd like that."

Holding the Bible to her chest, she turned to leave, letting Anna eat her dinner before it grew cold. As she locked the door behind her, she headed to her room to put the Bible down before finishing her last few chores. She found herself eager to read it. Could it really be for anyone like Anna said, even people like her?

***

Anna

Anna replayed the conversation as she ate dinner. Ella seemed interested in reading the Bible, which was encouraging. She hoped she did the right thing by not opening it with her the first time. She thought Ella might want to explore the Bible alone first before she shared the message of salvation with her. She didn't want to overwhelm her.

Sighing, she wished she could get Emery's advice on what to do. She didn't have much practice with sharing the gospel with people.

Emery was good at remembering verses without looking them up, whereas she had to mark them in order to find them when needed.

Thinking of Emery reminded Anna of the predicament she was in. She still didn't know why she was locked in, or why Emery's door had been locked. It seemed she had been waylaid in her quest for answers. Was it by divine purpose? Was she to use this time to help Ella?

She debated what to do. Should she try to get out when Ella brought one of the meals tomorrow? As the thought came to mind, she dismissed it just as quickly as she remembered the fear that haunted Ella's eyes. She didn't want to cause her undue harm. It looked like the best option was to wait, which wasn't exactly her forte.

Father, please help me to be patient and not rush into things like I normally do. Please help everything to be okay with Emery. Help me to know what to say to Ella about the Bible and You, and please show me what to do about being locked in.

Chapter 14

Anna

The next day passed at a snail pace for Anna. Out of boredom, she had slept the day away. Now she felt more energized than she had in a long time and was ready to do something. More importantly, she was ready to check on Emery.

A key turning in the lock pulled her attention to the door just in time to see Ella walk in. She smiled, happy to see her. She had been praying for guidance on how to help Ella see God's love for her.

Ella set the tray down and faced her. She seemed as if she wanted to say something but stood still, fidgeting with her hands. Anna waited, wanting her to start when she felt comfortable. She didn't have to wait long.

"What was it like growing up?"

Anna blinked, not expecting that question. She figured she would ask about God or something she had read from the Bible, not about her childhood.

"Well," she began, taking a seat on the bed. "I grew up in a small town called Riverbend. The houses there were much smaller than the one we're in now. I lived with my parents, and later Emery came to live with us."

She paused, remembering the sadness of those days. She couldn't imagine losing her parents and had been at a loss about how to help her friend. Thankfully, some ladies at church had stepped up, along with her parents, to help.

She glanced up and saw Ella studying her. Shaking those memories loose, she continued explaining what life was like in their small town, how it was going through school, her friendship with Emery, and the job she had worked before coming here.

The whole time she spoke, Ella remained silent. Again, Anna wondered about her story. As much as she wanted to know, she didn't want to push her away by asking too many questions. She hoped she would feel comfortable opening up soon.

Ella

While getting ready for bed that night, Ella pondered her conversation with Anna. From what she could tell, Anna was an ordinary girl like her. The thought gave her hope that maybe God really could love her and accept her like He did Anna.

Crawling under the covers, she thought about Anna and Emery's friendship. It sounded like they were very close. She was curious why Emery had moved in with Anna but hadn't asked when she saw Anna's eyes fill with sadness. Maybe she wasn't the only one with sadness marking her past.

Against her will, her thoughts drifted to her old friend group. Unlike Anna and Emery, they hadn't been overly close. At one time she had believed they were, but she had learned later that wasn't true.

Thinking of them brought up her mistake and the rumors. The reminder was like a slap in the face. What was she thinking? God couldn't love someone like her. Anna might appear ordinary, but she hadn't done anything bad. She didn't have black marks on her record.

Just when she grew hopeful, it was quickly snuffed out, like a flower forbidden to feel the warmth of sunshine. Discouragement began to take root.

She looked at the Bible beside her. She would need to give it back to Anna. She wished she didn't have to, but it was better to give it back before Anna started asking questions she wasn't ready to answer.

Anna

The chirping of birds marked the beginning of a new day. Anna took a minute to simply listen. Today was a new day, a day full of possibilities, and she was determined to see Emery. She couldn't wait another day to see if her friend was okay.

Noticing the time, she hurried to get dressed so she would be ready when Ella came with breakfast. She wanted to ask about Emery as soon as possible. She had barely finished getting ready when the sound of the door unlocking signaled Ella was here. Anna braced herself, hoping this went well.

When Ella came in, she noticed she was holding a book under her arm as she carried the tray. As she drew near, she saw it was her Bible. Why did she have it with her? Did she have questions about things she had read?

After putting the tray down, Ella held the Bible out to her. "I'm here to return this."

She felt her eyebrows rise. Had something happened to change things? "You don't want to keep it longer?" she asked.

Ella hesitated before shaking her head. Confused, she debated what to say. Ella seemed to take her silence as a request to leave because she set the Bible down beside the tray and turned to go.

"Wait!" she exclaimed.

Ella paused and slowly turned around.

"I hope I didn't offend you. Sometimes I get quiet when I'm thinking about something and lose track of how long I stay that way."

She saw relief flicker through Ella's eyes. "It's okay," she replied quietly as she started to head back to the door.

"Wait," Anna said again. "There's one more thing I would like to ask you."

Ella faced her more fully, waiting. She gulped, hoping this went well. "I would like to see Emery."

Shock and fear flashed across Ella's face. In a hurry to reassure her, she continued. "Please, I just want to check on her. I can't remember the last time I've seen her, and I'm starting to worry. I'm stronger now and feel up to the visit." She waited, pleading silently for Ella to grant her request.

She was surprised when tears formed in Ella's eyes. A sob broke free as Ella turned and ran for the door. Anna chased after her and caught her arm just as she gripped the door handle.

"Ella, please," she begged. "I don't understand what's going on or why I'm locked up, but I need to check on Emery. I don't want you to get in trouble though. If you can't take me to her, can you check on her for me?"

Ella only cried harder. Not sure what was upsetting her, she released her grip and moved her arm around Ella's shoulders, drawing her into a half hug. For a while, they simply stood there.

Eventually, Ella's sobs subsided. Anna let her arm fall as Ella drew herself away from her embrace. "I can't do this anymore," Ella stammered. "I can't follow through with it."

"Follow through with what?" she asked.

Ella wiped the remaining tears away, taking a deep breath. "I can't take you to see Emery because she's not here."

"What?" How could that be? If she wasn't here, where would she be?

"She's at the Sterling Manor."

Sterling, why did that name sound so familiar? Anna concentrated, trying to recall where she had heard it before. Then it hit her – Mr. Sterling had written to Emery offering his business advice in light of her uncle's passing. She didn't think Emery had planned to meet him.

"Why is she there?" she questioned.

Ella clutched her hands tightly together. "Mr. Sterling tricked her into coming and then…" She swallowed, her eyes darting to the side. She said the next part so softly Anna had to lean close to hear. "Mr. Sterling is forcing her to marry his son, so he can get Mr. Adler's business."

What? Of all things Ella could have said, that was the last thing she expected to hear. "I don't understand," she replied. "But regardless, Emery wouldn't agree to marry a stranger."

Ella lifted guilt reddened eyes to her. "She was told if she didn't marry his son, harm would come to you."

Anna's mind reeled. What did Mr. Sterling plan to do to her? She had never even met him.

"I understand if you hate me."

She turned to find Ella with her head down, staring at the floor. "Why would I hate you? You haven't done anything." *Well, besides locking me in*, she thought. Had she done so to keep her from going to Emery? Wait…if she knew about Emery, that meant…

"Ella," she said softly. "How did you know about Emery?" Ella glanced down, but not before Anna caught a glimpse of dread enter her eyes.

"Mr. Sterling placed me here as a spy. When he found out Mr. Adler had left everything to his niece, he began making plans to obtain the business." She pulled her gaze upward, looking Anna in the eye. "I'm so sorry." She sniffed. "I was instructed to slowly poison you until Emery is married to his son."

Anna stepped back. What was going on? She thought back to Ella's edginess. Then it hit her. "The cup," she stated. "That's how you did it wasn't it?"

Ella nodded. Anna's felt all jumbled inside. The realization she had been drinking poison sent a shiver through her. What kind of person would order such a thing done? She froze. The same person forcing her friend to marry his son.

She turned to Ella. "I need to get to Emery. Will you help me?"

Ella blinked. "What? You're asking me for help? But I…"

Anna came closer and laid her hand on Ella's arm. She felt her tense beneath her touch. "Ella," she said softly, "I don't hate you for what you did."

Ella's head jerked up searching her face. "You don't?"

Anna shook her head. "No, I'm guessing you were forced somehow to do what you did. You don't seem like the kind of person to purposefully hurt someone."

Ella's eyes turned misty. "Am I correct you were forced?" Anna asked.

Slowly, Ella nodded in response. "I didn't want to, but I felt like I didn't have a choice. I'm so sorry," she choked out.

"It's okay," Anna replied, giving her arm a gentle squeeze. "I'm better now. The important thing to focus on is Emery. Do you know when the wedding is supposed to be?"

The tears cleared from Ella's eyes as she responded, strength coming back into her voice. "I was instructed to poison you until Saturday, so I'm guessing the wedding is then."

Saturday, but that was only two days away! Anna began pacing. What was she going to do? How could she help her friend if she was locked in herself? She pushed down the rising panic. She needed to focus on finding a solution.

Please Father, show me what to do, she cried.

Her eyes caught on something outside. She walked towards the window. She gazed out but didn't see anything. It was then, standing by the window, that inspiration struck.

She had seen it done in movies; now it was time to see if she could do it herself. Looking down, she tried to estimate the distance.

It could work. Hope began blossoming in her chest as she faced Ella. "Do you think you could bring me extra bed sheets tonight?"

"What for?"

"I have an idea of how to help Emery. I've seen it done before." Anna decided to leave out the fact she had never done it herself. "I'm going to make a rope out of bed sheets and climb out the window once it gets dark."

She waited, hoping Ella would agree to help. After a while, she responded. "I can do that."

Anna breathed a sigh of relief. "Thank you so much." Excitement started to build as the plan took form. Noticing Ella's expression, she paused. "Ella, what will happen if you let me go?"

For a while, Ella said nothing. "Don't worry about me, Anna," she replied. "You have a friend that needs you more than me."

Anna took a step closer. "That doesn't mean I don't care what happens to you. Why don't you come with me?" She saw a war waging in Ella's eyes.

"I can't, but you go," she said. "I'll plan to bring the extra bed sheets at night with dinner. It wouldn't be questioned then since they would think you needed them before you retired for the evening."

Anna felt her heart swell at her willingness to help and her bravery to stay behind. "Thank you, Ella," she said. "This means a lot."

Ella gave a small smile in response before turning to leave. Anna stared after her until the door shut, the lock clicking in place. She hoped Ella would be okay. Maybe after she helped Emery she could come back to check on her. Anna walked back to the window.

Thank you, Father, she prayed. *Please help everything run smoothly. Help me to get to Emery in time. And please don't let Ella be punished for helping me.*

After she finished praying, she studied the landscape below, planning the best route for her escape.

Chapter 15

Mr. Sterling

Russell reclined in his office late into the evening, enjoying a bottle of whiskey as he celebrated his plan falling into place. Everything was running like a well-oiled machine. The seamstress had dropped off Emery's wedding dress in the afternoon, and Everett was due back some time this evening. He smiled to himself. Soon he would have James' business and could execute his plan, one that would make him a fortune.

An hour later he was halfway done with his bottle when there was a knock at the door. One of the staff entered and stood nervously by the entrance. "What?" he asked briskly, not wanting to be disturbed.

"Sir, there's someone here wanting to speak with you. He says it's urgent."

Russell sighed. "What is so urgent that it can't wait until tomorrow?"

The man wrung his hands. "I can't say for certain sir, but he said to tell you he was from the Adler estate."

He froze, straightening in his chair. "Send him in."

The man hurried to comply. Something must have happened. He reigned in his temper, working to portray a calm demeanor. A few minutes later the visitor eased the study door open and walked in.

Russell leaned forward. It wasn't the girl, but his other set of eyes at the estate. "What is it?" he asked.

As he listened to the man's tale, fury began to build inside of him. How could this happen? This could mess up everything!

He dismissed the man, telling him to send out search parties. Once he left, he fisted his fingers on his desk. He would not sit by and let his plans crumble around him. No one bested him, and this wasn't going to be the first.

Reaching inside a drawer, he pulled out some sheets of paper and began scribbling furiously on them. He rang for the house-keeper and instructed her to deliver them to Emery and Everett's rooms immediately. Once she left, he grabbed his phone and made a few calls.

Emery

Tears streamed down her face. She didn't have the energy to pray, couldn't form the words. She hunched over.

I feel so alone, she cried. *There's no one to help me, and now this.*

Her mind drifted to the note from Mr. Sterling. Just when she was beginning to climb the mountain, she was smacked back down. She felt as if she were drowning. Adrift at sea with no one to throw her a life saver.

She knew God was always there, but she couldn't feel His presence. It felt like her prayers bounced off the wall. Nothing penetrated the emotions holding her hostage.

Alone. Broken. The desire to feel whole, for life to return to how it was.

God, please take my burden. Please help me.

She sniffed, wiping her eyes as she curled deeper into her pillow. She folded her hands under her cheek, letting the tears continue to flow. She tried to focus her mind on God, on verses she knew from childhood, but nothing soaked in. Was her faith not strong enough? Was she doing something wrong? Why was she stuck in a hopeless situation?

You're not without hope when you have God.

Her mother's phrase wafted through her jumbled mind, puncturing a hole in the cloud hanging over her.

Oh, mother, she thought. *If only you were here to help me. To help me believe.*

Her parents always appeared so strong spiritually. Nothing seemed to get them down. She tried to be like them, but too often she fell short. Would she ever feel successful?

She pondered her mother's phrase. She knew it was true, yet how she felt didn't measure up. It was hard to cling to hope when all she saw were mountains. She felt as if she were lying to herself to believe she could overcome this. How could she fight against everything and everyone all at once?

It's not your battle to fight.

Again, one of her mother's pearls of wisdom rose above the noise. She knew it was based on a verse, but she couldn't recall the exact reference. Would God fight for her? She knew the stories from the Bible –David and Goliath, the men in the fiery furnace – but would He do the same for her?

She knew she shouldn't focus on the negative, but each time she tried to drag it to the positive, it swung back. She felt prompted to pray, but after having a prayer she cared so deeply about not answered how she had wanted a year ago, her prayers hadn't been the same. Her parents' absence had shaken her, and she hadn't fully gotten back to where she had been before.

God, I want to have hope, to let You fight for me. I'm just struggling to take the first step.

Emery closed her eyes, wanting to say more but not sure what to say. As her thoughts rolled back and forth against the shore of her mind, she clung to her mother's words of hope, praying for it to become real for her.

Emery jerked awake, her heart pounding. She looked around the room, trying to get her bearings. A resounding crack made her jump. Rain pelted the window, trying to hammer its way in. Lightning streaked the sky, highlighting the tempest outside. The raging winds howled with ferocity.

Amidst the storm, a voice sliced through the noise, forceful yet kind. WHY DON'T YOU TRUST ME?

Emery gripped the sides of her head, squeezing her eyes.

WHY?

Her chest tightened. *I'm scared*, she thought. *I don't know what will happen.*

YOU DON'T KNOW WHAT WILL HAPPEN NOW OR THE NEXT MINUTE. TRUST ME.

Emery placed her forehead in her hands, tears flowing down her cheeks. Why was it so hard?

Whenever she pictured taking a step of faith, her insides tightened, locking together, making her immobile. She knew verses about trust and faith, had heard songs about them growing up in church, and could even give others encouragement in their walk. But something held her back. Fear.

Fear of the unknown. Fear of getting hurt again.

She knew God was trustworthy. She knew He had her best interests in mind. But sometimes His ways didn't line up with hers. Sometimes He said no or allowed the hurt to penetrate. What if this was one of those times?

Nothing was working out. Everett had hardly been here this week, leaving her without someone to help her plan an escape. She hadn't seen Anna since the dreadful note that started all this. Had she succumbed to the poison? Then her discovery in the library left her on pins and needles. And now, to top it off, the wedding had been moved up to tomorrow.

A fresh wave of tears hit. She couldn't see a light at the end of the tunnel. If God was her source of hope, where was He? Why did He show up for other people and not her? She had already lost her parents. She couldn't lose Anna and everything she knew.

TRUST ME.

She wanted to. She really did. But taking that leap felt like stepping off a cliff.

TRUST ME.

The phrase wouldn't leave her mind, replaying as if on repeat.

Emery pushed herself to her feet and began pacing, trying to outrun the voice, the conviction. She thought again of Anna. Anna wasn't afraid to take a leap of faith. Sometimes she wished she was more like her friend, ready to jump at a moment's notice.

Now when she wanted to escape the troubles surrounding her, sleep eluded her. She closed her eyes at another crack of thunder, trying to still her rapidly beating heart. Storms had always unnerved her. The power invoked a terror inside of her, making her feel small and helpless.

Her eyes welled up. It seemed she was always crying lately. Her life was falling apart around her, and tomorrow's wedding would be the final nail in the coffin.

Why God? she cried. *Why is this happening?*

She dropped her head in her hands, letting the storm inside run its course. It was then, in the midst of the angst, a verse from Hebrews came to mind.

"I will never leave you nor forsake you."

Her sobs stilled. She waited. Nothing else came, but a measure of peace wrapped itself around her in its warm embrace. God was with her. She was not alone.

Lifting her head, she wiped her eyes and headed to the bed, reaching for her Bible. She flipped through the pages, not entirely sure what to look for but knew she needed it.

She landed in the book of Matthew and saw the heading "Jesus Calms the Storm." It seemed appropriate. She began to read the passage out loud.

As she did, the most surreal thing happened. Outside the storm continued to beat against the windows, but inside she felt calm. The inkling of peace she had felt earlier grew to encompass her whole heart. She waited, listening to the wind and rain battle it out, yet the peace inside remained.

A smile slowly bloomed across her face. She had heard of God's word being alive and active, and now she was experiencing it herself. The storm outside hadn't changed, but she was calm on the inside. Her circumstances hadn't changed, yet she was at peace. The God of the Bible is still the same God today. Just as He calmed the stormy seas back then, He can do the same today.

Reflecting on God's character brought fresh tears to her eyes. This time though, they weren't a product of sorrow. They were in response to God's goodness, His faithfulness, His love. His love for her.

The reminder of His love caused her to bow her head. How could she forget such a thing? Her circumstances didn't determine His love for her. Sorrow, pain, and fear didn't erase His love.

I'm so sorry, God she cried. *I let my situation overshadow what I know to be true. Bad things don't mean You don't love me. You said in this world we would have trouble, so how can I expect only good things? But You're with us through it all, even in the storms of life.*

She paused, letting her mind soak everything in. Her tears stilled. The peace remained. Slowly, she wiped the wetness away and lifted her head. Was she ready to take the leap, to step off the cliff in faith?

The thought still caused an inkling of fear to surface, but it didn't override the peace. God didn't promise a smooth way in life or to reveal every detail, but He had proven Himself trustworthy. Her mind drifted to Anna. If she could trust a friend, she could trust in God. He was in control. Nothing could happen to her without Him allowing it.

Taking a deep breath, Emery let it out slowly, contemplating the idea of faith. The definition from Hebrews came to mind – believing in what you can't see. It was as if she was seeing things through fresh eyes.

It wasn't faith if you could see it. You had to believe and trust. Just like she couldn't see God, yet believed He was real. Nature pointed to His very existence. How else could someone explain the complexity of the human body or the breath-taking beauty of a sunset?

If evidence pointed to this reality, why did she ignore the evidence of God's sovereignty and love? The fact He sent His one and only Son to die for her sins that she may live with Him spoke to the depth of His love for her.

He may allow pain and sadness, but His love remains steadfast. She had to trust His ways because He could see the whole picture. She could trust in Him and His love for her. The verse from Proverbs that had played through her mind the past week came to the forefront of her thoughts again.

"Trust in the Lord will all your heart and lean not on your own under-standing. In all your ways acknowledge Him and He will make your paths straight."

Emery repeated the verse to herself. Trust in the Lord with all your heart. With all your heart.

I trust You, God she prayed. *I'm choosing to trust You.*

A weight she didn't realize she was carrying lifted off her shoulders. She felt light, free. Smiling, she savored the feeling.

After some time, she gently closed her Bible and returned it to the nightstand. She noticed the storm had ceased, a soft rain tapping the window in its place. Laying her head on the pillow, she allowed her eyes to drift closed. In what seemed like a long time, she slept in peace.

Chapter 16

Ella

Ella stirred and opened her eyes to see the dawn breaking on the horizon. She took a moment to study the majesty of the painted sky. It almost made her forget the troubles of last night. She turned to check on Anna and found her sleeping. She was glad to see she had finally been able to rest, however good one could rest enclosed in shrubbery.

Pushing herself to a sitting position, her muscles groaned in protest after sleeping on the unforgiving, damp ground. Stretching her aching muscles, her mind wandered back to last night.

She had agreed to help Anna with her plan to escape and had brought extra bed sheets to her room with dinner. Anna had asked her to come with her once more, but as tempting as the offer was, she couldn't accept. She hadn't wanted to put Anna in more danger than she was already in. But her plans had changed when she saw Anna fall.

The bed sheets had proven too short of a rope, so Anna decided to drop the last few feet. Ella heard her cry out before she crumbled in a heap on the ground. She had waited for Anna to move, but when she hadn't, she made the choice to follow her through the window.

Letting go of the bed sheets had been daunting, but she stuck the landing and was able to half carry, half drag Anna to some shrubbery nearby. She had wanted to be further away before morning, but each time she moved Anna she moaned. Not wanting to inflict more pain, she had stopped behind a hedge of shrubs.

Now with morning coloring the sky, Ella pondered what to do next. If Anna was feeling better, they might be able to get her some help. Surely someone nearby would be willing to offer some aid. A rustling made her pause. Crouching low to the ground, she inched her way to the gap in the nearest shrub.

When she looked out, she saw a handful of the staff walking around the grounds by Anna's bedroom window. The bed sheet rope still hung from the window, billowing softly in the breeze. Her heart pounded. In light of Anna's injury, she had forgotten about their escape rope.

Even without the rope, the alarm should have alerted the chief of staff when they dropped from the window. Unless, she thought, it hadn't been set yet. With Mr. Adler no longer alive, she wasn't sure how vigilant the security was being kept.

Noticing some men glance up, she followed their gaze from a distance, wondering what they were looking at. Then it hit her, the security cameras. She bit her lip. They would definitely make out two people on the footage, but how far did the cameras go?

Seeing those same men venture their way, she quietly backed up and crawled to where Anna lay asleep. Anna stirred as if sensing her presence. She laid a hand on her shoulder to calm her and felt Anna grow still again.

The snapping of twigs sent her heart racing as she bent closer to Anna. *Please don't find us*, she thought. *Just keep walking*.

The crunching of leaves underfoot grew louder. Ella squeezed her eyes shut, hoping with everything she had they wouldn't be discovered. After a few moments passed, she slowly reopened her eyes. The sound of footsteps continued to grow softer.

She released her breath slowly, relief flowing through her. She moved a little ways from Anna and sat quietly, listening to the sounds around her and occasionally taking a peak through the gap in the shrubbery. It appeared they had moved on or given up the search for now, but she needed to move Anna quickly.

Hearing movement behind her, she turned to see Anna waking up and hurried over to her. "How are you feeling?" she asked as Anna pushed herself up, grimacing.

"Okay, I think," Anna replied.

Ella glanced at her ankle. She hadn't been able to see how bad her injury was in the dark last night. "How is your ankle?"

She watched as Anna gingerly rolled up her pant leg. Her stomach turned at the sight of Anna's swollen ankle sporting black and blue splotches. She gazed up. Anna took a shaky breath. "Can you help me stand?"

What? Standing on her ankle seemed like the last thing she should be doing. But before she could tell her that, Anna was already trying to pull herself upright using the nearest shrub for support. Not wanting her to injure herself even further, she scrambled to her feet and hurried to help her.

She wrapped one arm around her back and clasped one of Anna's arms with her other hand. "On three," she told Anna. At the count of three, she lifted as Anna tried to push herself up using her good leg.

Grunting, Ella bent lower to get more momentum. With one last heave, Anna was upright, but leaning heavily against her, her breathing ragged. "You okay?" she asked Anna, breathing hard from the exertion as well. A few seconds passed before Anna nodded.

She felt Anna's weight lift slightly off her as she attempted to put weight on her other leg. Ella braced herself, ready to catch Anna if her ankle gave out.

Anna had only managed a few steps before she stumbled. Ella wasn't able to fully counter the sudden drop and ended up slowing their fall to the ground more than catching her.

Anna buried her face in her hands. "What am I going to do now?" she cried. "I can't walk far with my ankle like this. How am

I going to help Emery? Today is Friday, which means the wedding is tomorrow."

Anna lifted her head and stared off into the distance as if waiting for a solution to drop from the sky. Ella remained quiet, not sure what to say to make it better.

After a while, Anna turned back, her eyebrows scrunched slightly. "If I could just get to a car, then I could make it to Emery." A light began to enter her eyes.

Ella hesitated, not wanting to shatter her newfound hope. "But what would you do when you got to the Sterling Manor?"

Anna's face fell. "You're right," she whispered. "It still doesn't change the fact I can't walk far."

Ella's heart ached for Anna. She knew she and Emery were close friends after listening to Anna's stories about her childhood. It was partly because of those heartfelt stories she had given in and told Anna Mr. Sterling's plan to marry Emery off to his son.

She had known the risk she was taking doing so, yet she couldn't keep it to herself any longer. She already had enough marks against her. She didn't need another.

Now with Anna hurt, she contemplated what to do. Her breathing slowed when she realized there was only one choice. The thought of approaching Sterling Manor nearly paralyzed her. If caught, how would she explain her presence there? Did Mr. Sterling already know Anna was missing?

The questions did little to lessen the fear coursing through her. It was one thing to aid Anna in her escape out the window, it was an entirely different thing to try and help Emery escape.

A touch on her arm brought her back to the present. Glancing down, she saw Anna looking at her in concern. Seeing it caused tears to form. Here she was scared for herself, and Anna was worried about her. Anna, the one with a hurt ankle and friend in need, was worried about her. Ella let the tears flow down her cheeks.

She felt Anna's weight shift before hands gripped both of her arms. "Ella, what's wrong?"

She looked up, meeting Anna's green gaze, but couldn't get any words to take form. Anna pulled her into a hug. Within her warm embrace, the last of her resolve shattered. Never before had someone cared for her like this. Never before had she known this kind of love from another person. Love that reflected genuine care.

When her tears stopped, she pulled herself from Anna's embrace, partly reluctant to leave. Anna's face seemed to plead with her to tell her what was wrong. So, it was there, in the middle of a hedge of shrubbery on the wet ground, that she decided to open herself up to friendship again.

Wiping her cheeks, she took a deep breath, trying not to lose her nerve. "I'm sorry," she said. "But when I saw your concern, I couldn't hold it back."

Anna's forehead crinkled. "What do you mean?"

Ella took another breath before continuing. "I was thinking about our next step when I realized the only option would be for me to go." She paused, weary of admitting her own selfish thoughts or weaknesses, but pressed on.

"The thought of going to Mr. Sterling's house filled me with such terror I couldn't think straight. Then I looked at you and saw concern for me." Her voice broke.

"No one has cared for me like that before. Here you are, your ankle hurt and your best friend in trouble, yet you were worried about me." She shook her head, unable to say any more.

"Oh, Ella," said Anna, reaching over to touch her arm. Ella saw tears forming in her eyes. "I am so sorry you've felt unloved, but there is One who loves and cares about you even more than me."

She stared back, wondering who could possibly love her that much.

"God loves you Ella and always has."

She shook her head, wanting to believe it but knowing it couldn't be true.

"It's true," said Anna. "God created you and loves you. He loves you so much He sent His son Jesus to die for you."

Anna didn't know everything about her. "It's not possible," she told Anna. "God couldn't love someone like me."

"Why do you think that?" Anna asked softly.

Ella looked down. "Trust me," she whispered. "I'm not like you."

Anna shook her head. "No one is perfect, Ella. God welcomes anyone who comes to Him through His Son."

Oh, how she wished it were true. "Not this time," she replied sadly.

Ella felt the pressure on her arm lift as Anna twisted and reached for something off to the side. With a grunt, she turned back around with her bag in her hand. She rummaged inside and pulled out her Bible and began flipping through the pages. Ella watched as she went from one tab to another.

Finally, she stopped and held the Bible out to her. She pointed to a verse that was underlined. "Read this verse. It's from John 6:37."

Taking hold of the Bible, Ella laid it in her lap and looked at the verse Anna referred to. As she read it, she felt hope begin to blossom in her chest. Could it be true?

She reread it again before pulling her gaze up to meet Anna's. "Is it true?" she asked.

Anna smiled and nodded.

But before her newfound hope could grow a new thought entered her mind. "What about things we've done wrong? Can God forgive any sin, even the bad ones?"

"We sometimes think of some sins as worse than others, but it's still sin. And all sin separates us from God," Anna replied. "But if you confess your sins to Him, He will forgive you."

The idea of all sin being bad hadn't occurred to her before. She figured some sins were too bad and therefore unforgivable. She chewed her lip, wondering how much to tell Anna. What if she ran away like her other friends?

"Ella."

She looked up and saw compassion in Anna's eyes. "Would you like to tell me what is weighing you down? We can share the burden together."

Fear and uncertainty waged against each other, but the compassion she saw in Anna's face won out. Looking down at her lap, she told Anna what had kept her shackled for so long.

"About a year ago, I was hanging out with some friends. There were four of us. Cora was the leader of the group and had turned twenty-one. She threw a big party at her house to celebrate, inviting all the cool people. Her house was huge compared to mine, and I figured she would pack it full of people. I'm not a fan of large crowds, but I didn't want to appear weak. I thought I was lucky they included me in their friend group to begin with and didn't want to jeopardize that."

She paused, gathering her courage before continuing. "Part of me wished my mother would say I couldn't go, but she wasn't around since she is always working." Taking a breath, she kept going.

"When I got there, music was already blaring, and a crowd of people were already crammed inside. I wanted to run away right then, but instead I stepped inside and pushed my way through the throng to find my friends."

"When I found them, they were talking with a group of people I vaguely recalled seeing before. They had drinks in their hands and offered me one. With multiple eyes on me, I didn't want to ostracize myself, so I took one, telling myself I wouldn't drink it, just hold it." She gazed off into the distance, memories of that night flooding back.

"I hung back in a corner most of the night, trying not to draw attention to myself and wishing I was somewhere else. As the evening wore on, people moved furniture to the edges of the rooms to clear space for a dance floor."

"After some time, a guy approached and asked if I wanted to dance. I panicked and looked around for my friends, but they were too caught up in having fun to notice. Seeing them made me wish I could relax and have fun like that too, so I agreed to the dance. One dance led to another and before I knew it, a lot of time had passed." The memory of what came next felt as fresh as it did back then.

"The guy I was dancing with said he wanted to show me something and led me to a secluded spot away from the crowd. He had taken me to the library. I was wondering what we were doing there when he kissed me."

"At first, I was too shocked to move, but then he got more aggressive, and I started to panic. I jerked and tried to get away." The terror she had felt then resurfaced, but Anna's touch on her arm chased the feelings away.

Keeping her eyes in the distance, she continued. "He was strong. The more I struggled, the tighter his grip seemed to be. Just when I was beginning to lose all hope, there was a commotion outside, and he backed off. I stumbled away and frantically looked for a way to run past while his back was to me."

"When he turned around to face me again, I froze, afraid. His gaze looked me up and down before he smirked and walked away, saying he was going to look for better entertainment elsewhere." The relief, hurt, and disgust from the moment felt as real as it had then. She swallowed, willing herself to finish the story.

"I took a few minutes to gather myself before leaving the room. I hadn't made it far when I bumped into Cora. Relief flowed through me at the sight of a familiar face. I began to tell her what had happened. When I was done, she shook her head, pity painted across her face." Ella swallowed.

"She told me I was a hopeless case, claiming she had done me a favor by sending the guy over. She said if I couldn't appreciate what she had done, or impress him enough to stick around, then I wasn't up to being her friend. She stated she only hung out with the best."

Again, the betrayal felt just as raw as it had then. "I chased after her, and finally caught up with her as she neared our other friends. She held out her hand, stopping me. I told her she wasn't making any sense, but she turned back to the people around her."

Anna gently squeezed her arm. "Ella, look at me."

She was reluctant to look, not wanting to see the same disappointment that had marked her friends' faces.

"Please, Ella."

After taking a deep breath and letting it out slowly, she opened her eyes and turned to face Anna. Instead of disgust, she saw the same compassion she had earlier. Her eyes welled up.

"Ella, you do not have to be the person those girls wanted you to be."

She swallowed back her tears. "It doesn't matter," she said. "Tons of people were at the party and think otherwise. Word spread no guy would have me. Whenever I went out in public, I was met with pity or subjected to snide comments. My mother never found out though. At least her jobs kept her busy."

"But you didn't do anything," Anna stated.

She shook her head, appreciating Anna's defense, but feeling unworthy of it.

Anna gripped her hand. "Ella, you are so much more than the image your friends paint you to be. You don't have to be the person they say you are. You don't have to try to impress people to be their friends. Real friends look out for you and love you the way you are."

Anna spoke with such conviction it was easy to believe her. She knew Anna was right. She had already come to the conclusion Cora and the others weren't true friends, but that only left her empty. She hadn't made any new friends since the incident.

As if sensing her downward thoughts, Anna spoke again. "You are special and unique, Ella."

She almost laughed at the thought but didn't have time before Anna continued.

"You are created and loved by God. He loves you so much He made a way for you to be with Him forever. Do you believe this?"

She paused, considering Anna's words. She wanted to believe them, but something held her back. "That all sounds good Anna, but I'm no one special," she said. "I didn't have much growing up and spent most of my time alone. When I found a friend group in high school, I felt better for a time, but then the emptiness soon returned."

"There's nothing about me that would catch God's attention. Besides, I have a reputation after Cora's party that follows me around. How could God forgive or even love someone believed to have something wrong with her? I'm not perfect like you."

Anna shook her head. "I'm not perfect either. I sin and make bad choices just like everyone else."

Ella looked at her, sputtering. "But you go to church and read the Bible."

"Yes," Anna said. "But that doesn't make me perfect. We are all sinners in need of God's grace and forgiveness. Sin is what separates us from God because He is holy. We all need Jesus to save us because there's nothing we can do on our own to make ourselves clean."

Anna took her hand again. "God made a way for you, me, and everyone to be saved. John 3:16 says God loved the world so much He gave His only Son, Jesus, and that those who believe in Him won't perish but have eternal life. Jesus died on the cross to take your sins and the sins of the whole world off our shoulders and onto His."

"He took the punishment we deserved. We deserve judgment for the sins we commit, but He stepped into our place and three days later rose from the grave. Death couldn't keep ahold of Him, and He lives today, wanting others to be saved and come to Him."

As Ella listened, she felt as if her eyes and heart were opening. The more Anna talked, the more she wanted to believe God truly loved her and would forgive her for all the things she had done wrong, all the ways she had fallen short.

"Salvation is a gift from God," Anna said. "Ephesians 2:8 tells us it's by grace we have been saved, through faith. God offers this free gift to everyone. And those who accept it are made new in Jesus."

The thought of being made new, having a clean start, appealed to her. The idea of not being portrayed as the girl she had been felt like a dream. A dream she desperately wanted to make a reality. "How do I get this gift?"

Anna reached over and took the Bible from her lap, turning to another marked page before handing it back to her. "Read Acts 16:31."

Ella did as she said. As she read, the words seemed to speak directly to her. It was as if the clouds had finally parted from her mind, and she could see clearly. She looked at Anna.

"Ella, do you believe Jesus died for your sins and rose again? Do you want to ask Him to be your Savior?"

Tears filled her eyes as she nodded her head yes. Anna smiled and took her hand. "I'll say a sample prayer and pause for you to insert your own words as you pray it yourself."

Ella gripped Anna's hand in return and bowed her head. As she prayed, she felt lightness spread its way inside of her. It continued to flow until it filled every nook and cranny, every vein of her existence. Finally, after so long, she felt free. She felt loved.

Chapter 17

Emery

Emery woke to sunshine pouring through the window, chasing away the remnants from last night's storm. She smiled. The feeling of peace she had felt last night was still with her this morning.

Thank you for reminding me You can bring good from bad. That You're with me in the storm.

A knock at the door announced the housekeeper's arrival as she carried in a breakfast tray with a note. Emery picked up the note and began reading it as the housekeeper silently departed. Like the others, the note was short and to the point.

The pastor will be in the receiving room at 10:00 am.

The housekeeper will help you dress at 9:00 am and escort you to the room.

Glancing at the clock, she saw it read 8:15. Less than two hours of freedom left. Fear started banging on the door of her heart, wanting to take root. She laid the note on the tray and grabbed her Bible. Leaning back against the pillows, she closed her eyes.

God, if it is Your will, please help me find a way out of this marriage. I'm choosing to trust You despite how bleak it looks. I know You can stop it if You choose. Please show me what to do.

As she sat quietly, trying not to let fear make its way to the surface, the story of Esther came to mind. Opening her eyes, she turned to the book of Esther and started reading.

As she read, she couldn't help but think of her own situation. Esther had been chosen to marry the king just like Mr. Sterling had chosen her for his son. Emery wondered how Esther had felt during the process. Had she been afraid? Did she resent being forced into such a position?

Emery thought of her own situation. She knew Mr. Sterling was not to be taken lightly given his propensity to poison or kill to get his way. She had no doubt he would follow through on his threat against Anna if she backed out of the wedding. Not wanting to dwell any further on that, she turned back to Esther and kept reading. When she reached chapter six, she paused.

At the end of chapter five, Haman had devised a plan to have Mordecai impaled on a pole he had set up the next day. Chapter six started with, "That night the king could not sleep; so he ordered the book of the chronicles, the record of his reign, to be brought in and read to him."

It just so happened the king discovered Mordecai hadn't been honored for saving his life once, so the next day he was led throughout the city in honor by none other than Haman. Afterwards, Haman attended a banquet with Esther and the king where Esther presented her request to save her people. When the king found out Haman was behind it, he ordered him impaled on the same pole he had erected for Mordecai.

Looking up from her Bible, Emery reflected on the chapters she had read, especially chapters six and seven. Things weren't looking good for the Jews or Mordecai, even right up to the day Haman planned to kill Mordecai. But God had a plan, and His plan prevailed over man's. Haman planned Mordecai's demise, yet God turned things around before disaster struck.

Again, she thought of her situation. She was set to marry Everett in less than two hours because of the evil planned by a man named Mr. Sterling. After reading Esther, she was reminded that ultimately,

God is in control. The reassurance of His sovereignty was like a balm, soothing in its touch.

God came through in time to save Mordecai and the Jews, and He could do the same for her. With this thought in mind, Emery started in on her breakfast before the housekeeper returned to help her dress.

Ella

Ella steeled herself as she hid behind a tree. It had only been a few minutes since she had left Anna safely hidden in the greenhouse at the edge of the property and already, she was beginning to lose her nerve. She didn't like the idea of leaving Anna alone, but if no one had found them yet, she figured Anna was safe until she got back. If she got back.

No, she wasn't going to think that way. She was not the same person she had been the past week, or even the past year. She now knew God loved her and cared about her.

Anna explained after their prayer earlier she was now a child of God and that they were sisters in the faith. She wasn't sure entirely what that meant, but she liked the sound of it. After everything Anna had done for her, the least she could do was try to help her in return.

Closing her eyes as she leaned against the tree, she felt the rough bark pinch her skin through her shirt. She willed her mind to focus.

God, I know I'm new to this, and I'm not sure what the right words are to say, but would You please help me do the task before me? I need to reach Emery and try to help her escape, or at the very least tell her Anna is safe. Speaking of Anna, can You please help her ankle to feel better soon and keep her safe while I am gone?

She paused, wondering what else she should say. Nothing came to mind, so after a deep breath, she opened her eyes, peeked around the corner, and started off in the direction of the Sterling Manor.

Emery

Emery tried to present a calm exterior, not wanting Mr. Sterling to get any satisfaction from today. For most of the morning she had felt calm, but now that she found herself standing outside the receiving room, she couldn't keep her heart from increasing its rhythm.

The thought of marriage hadn't crossed her mind before. In fact, she had resigned herself to remaining single with her books for company. Now here she was, about to marry a complete stranger, so Mr. Sterling could obtain her late uncle's company. For a person who liked to know the future, never in her wildest dreams did she envision this.

After glancing at the clock, the housekeeper took her arm and ushered her into the room. As she entered, she noted it looked the same as before, no flowers or décor of any kind littered the room. It seemed the only indicators a wedding was about to take place was the pastor standing in front of the fireplace and the white dress she was wearing.

It seemed the only expense Mr. Sterling deemed necessary was a dress for her. She wore a poofy dress that breathed elegance from the fabric to the intricate design and beadwork woven throughout it. It was a dress fit for a princess, except this was no fairytale and there was no prince charming waiting at the end of the aisle.

Sooner than she wanted, she found herself facing Everett with the pastor in her peripheral vision. Like herself, Everett was decked out in the finest wearing a smartly tailored suit. He could almost be considered handsome if it wasn't for his gloomy air.

Though his face remained impassive, his eyes held resignation, as if he were standing before a judge ready to receive his sentence. The imagery would have made her laugh if the situation wasn't so dire. As the pastor began talking, her heart increased its beating.

God, I'm trusting You. I read in Esther this morning how You came through for Mordecai, please do the same for me. Please.

Her prayer died out as she held back tears. She would not cry. She would face whatever came with God by her side.

Despite the brave words, an inkling of fear remained nestled in her spine. She kept repeating the verse from last night – "Trust in the Lord with all your heart." Trust in Him.

Ella

Ella stood facing the Sterling Manor. It looked as intimating as its owner. *You can do this*, she told herself. *You've come this far. Don't give up now.*

As she stood staring at the house, she said another quick prayer. *Okay, God, I'm here. Please show me what to do.*

Taking a deep breath for courage, she raised her hand to the knocker and waited, attempting to school her features. The plan she had thought up on the way here was straightforward. She knew she couldn't make it too complicated, or she would never remember it. She was simply going to request to see Mr. Sterling and then act panic stricken when she told him Anna had escaped.

The panicking part shouldn't be too hard to pull off when she was standing in front of the man himself. After that, she wasn't sure what would happen. She had planned to wait and see how Mr. Sterling reacted before deciding what to do next.

When no one answered the door, she tried the knocker once more. Again, she was met with silence. She paused, her thoughts beginning to race. It wasn't normal for a butler not to answer a door, especially one that worked for a taskmaster like Mr. Sterling. Glancing to either side and seeing no one, she decided to take a quick look around.

Crouching down, she crept along the outside of the house, peeking in windows when she could. Nothing so far.

Just as she was thinking she should stop and regroup, movement in the window ahead caught her eye. She approached slowly, not wanting to draw attention to herself.

As she neared the bushes outside the window, her breath caught in her throat at the sight before her. Two people impeccably dressed, for a wedding no less, stood before what looked to be a pastor. What was going on? The wedding was supposed to be tomorrow!

She slipped back down, trying to think quickly. What was she going to do? Should she barge in and try to stop the wedding? Just as quickly as she thought it, she dismissed the idea. That would more likely see her behind bars than help Emery.

Come on, think, she told herself. But the sense of urgency was clouding her thinking. In desperation she cried out to God.

Suddenly, she became aware of the weight on her back. Reaching behind her, she took off the bag Anna had packed when she planned her escape out the window. Opening the bag, she dug around inside, looking for anything that might help her.

She pulled out clothes, pens, and a Bible. Hanging her head in despair, she tried to hold the tears at bay. She was so close to Emery, but they might as well be worlds apart for all the good it did.

She reached for the items before her, intending to put them back, when her hands stilled over the Bible. An idea began to take shape in her mind. It seemed a little far-fetched, but at this point she would try anything. She quickly put the plan in motion, praying it would work.

Chapter 18

Emery

*D*espite her earlier bravery, Emery couldn't keep from breaking out in a sweat. It was getting harder to stay hopeful that God would intervene when the pastor finished his speech and was starting on the vows. It was all she could do to keep the panic from showing. Was God going to stop it? Could she really go through with it if He didn't?

TRUST ME.

The words punctured the panic blanketing her heart. Breathing in, she repeated the words to herself. Good or bad, married or not, she needed to trust God.

Her newfound resolve in place, she straightened her spine and looked at Everett. As she did, something out of the corner of her eye caught her attention. Shifting her eyes slightly to the left, she saw someone squeezed between two bushes holding something up.

At first, she was too stunned at the sight to comprehend anything. What was someone doing lurking around Mr. Sterling's manor? This was the last place anyone should be sneaking around. Squinting, she guessed it to be a woman.

The person waved something in her hands. Focusing on the object, Emery tried to get a better glimpse. It appeared to be a book. Why was this person holding a book?

Her confusion must have shown because the person jerked the book down, frantically opened it, and held it back up, gesturing to something written in large print on the inside cover. The writing filled the whole page, and what she read stopped her cold. What did this mean? Was it a sign?

She looked at it again, half believing it was a mirage and would disappear. But it was still there. In large lettering, the name 'Anna' was written with a check mark beside it. Did that mean Anna was okay? But if so, how?

Emery's mind churned with questions, racing to come up with a conclusion. Before she could, the sound of a throat clearing drew her attention back to the present. She glanced to the pastor and saw him staring at her.

"I'm sorry," she said. "Did you say something?"

"I asked if you would take this man to be your lawfully wedded husband."

She gulped and turned to face Everett. His earlier resignation was lined with curiosity. Had he noticed her mind had wandered? Had anyone else noticed? Chewing her lip, she chanced another subtle peek towards the window. The person still held the book opened to Anna's name.

God, is this a sign? Is this You showing me a way out?

She looked again at Everett, then at Mr. Sterling off to the right. Did she take the chance? If it was true, Mr. Sterling wouldn't have anything to hold over her. But if she guessed wrong, she didn't want to imagine the consequences that would follow.

When she noticed impatience cross Mr. Sterling's features, she quickly turned back to Everett. She needed to make a decision. It was now or never.

She took a deep breath, trying to gather her thoughts. Her heart raced with anticipation. She opened her mouth to speak, but her voice came out scratchy. Clearing her throat, she tried again. "I...don't."

Ella

The tension was almost more than Ella could take. Her arms bore scratches from being sandwiched between two thorny bushes, but she couldn't leave yet. Had Emery been able to read her writing?

She thought she had detected recognition in her eyes, but Emery hadn't looked her way again in a while. She kept looking off to the side and then back to the man in front of her.

She was debating whether to risk knocking on the window when she saw Emery back away. She leaned closer. She saw Mr. Sterling advancing on Emery. Everett stepped between them. They appeared to engage in a heated conversation.

She glanced in Emery's direction and their gazes locked. Ella jerked her head to the side, motioning for her to leave. Emery seemed to understand because she took a few small steps back before making a beeline for the doorway.

Emery didn't make it far though before a staff member blocked her exit. Seeing Mr. Sterling go around his son and head Emery's way, she knew she needed a diversion. Before she could give it much thought, she started banging on the window, making as much ruckus as she could.

All eyes turned her way. She focused her attention on the men, hoping Emery could find a way past the person blocking her. Mr. Sterling took a step her way, his face the color of molten lava. She could easily imagine fire spewing out of his mouth.

After a few steps, something drew his attention backwards. Ella followed his gaze and saw Emery and the staff member gone. Not wanting to stick around, she muscled her way out of the bush and headed towards the front entrance.

As she ran, she quickly stuffed the Bible back in the bag and slung it over her shoulders. Ignoring her stinging arms from the bush's scratches, she bolted towards the front door, not caring if anyone saw her.

Just as she rounded the corner, Emery burst through the front door. Not taking time to speak or introduce herself, she grabbed Emery's hand and took off in the direction of Anna.

Mr. Sterling

A thud ricocheted throughout the room as items rattled on the shelves. Russell stormed to his desk, brewing like a pot set to boil over. So close! He had been so close to clinching the deal before that slip of a girl ruined it.

Who did she think she was that she thought to defy him? He wasn't sure what made her change her mind, but she would pay, both her and her friend. And Ella. When he got a glimpse of her through the window, he was livid. No one crossed him and got away with it.

Russell yanked open the bottom drawer, lifted the flap concealing the hidden compartment, and took out the key. Shoving everything back into place, he set off towards the library, rage fueling his steps. He would show those girls not to mess with the great Russell Sterling.

He neared his destination in record time. Walking briskly through the shelves of books, he stopped before one particular shelf towards the back of the library. He reached for a book and gave it a quick yank, barely waiting for the shelf to swing inward before squeezing into the room.

The room was dimly lit, but he didn't need any help finding what he was looking for. He stopped before a row of cabinets above a desk, his eyes skipping over the skull and crossbones to the bottles labeled with the letter z. Grabbing one, he shoved it into his pocket.

As he left the library, he mentally ticked off the items on his to do list. Time was of the essence if he wanted to salvage this disaster before it was too late. He needed to change into more suitable clothing, recruit Everett's aid, and ensure word didn't get out about what had transpired. He was not a man who failed, and he wasn't about to start now.

Emery

Gasping for air, Emery stumbled blindly after the girl in front of her. She didn't know her name, but trusted she was leading her to Anna. A stitch developed in her side. As she clutched her side to alleviate the pain, she couldn't help but think when this was all over, she needed to start running.

She attempted to keep her dress off the ground the best she could as she followed the girl on foot, thankful she wasn't wearing heels during this mad dash through the outskirts of town.

Her breathing became more ragged, making her sound like a fish out of water. Just as she felt on the verge of collapse, the girl veered to the side and ducked behind some bushes and trees.

She forced her feet to keep moving, pushing her way through the greenery to the other side. Leaning against a tree, she doubled over, gasping for air. She would have kissed the ground in joy if she thought she would have the strength to get back up.

As her breaths grew less ragged, she glanced up to see the girl with her back against a nearby tree. Her blonde locks clung in wet tendrils to her forehead. Something about her looked familiar.

When she was confident her breathing was level enough to speak, Emery straightened. "What's your name?"

"Ella."

"Is what you wrote about Anna true? Is she really okay?" she asked, both hopeful and weary.

"Well, yes and no," Ella said.

"What do you mean?"

Ella pushed away from the tree. "She's no longer being poisoned, but she hurt her ankle trying to escape to come find you."

"Find me?" she questioned. "How did she know?"

Ella looked at the ground, shuffling her feet. "I told her." She said quietly.

Emery sensed there was more to the story but decided it could wait until later. "Well, however she found out, I'm just glad she's no longer being poisoned. Where is she?"

Ella turned and looked off in the distance. "She's not much farther," she replied, turning back around. "I helped her hide in the greenhouse on your uncle's property before leaving to find you."

"Okay, lead on," she said. "We should keep going." Ella seemed to hesitate a moment before nodding and heading off again. As she followed, Emery took a moment to give thanks as she walked along.

Chapter 19

Anna

Anna's ankle throbbed as she shifted in the chair. Gritting her teeth, she forced herself to remain still. Why did her ankle have to be injured now? The one time her friend desperately needed her, she was stuck in a greenhouse, unable to help.

She wasn't sure how much time had passed, but it felt like too long. Where were they? Had something happened? Ella should have been back with Emery by now. She hung her head in frustration, tears threatening to surface. It was torture to not be able to help her friend, but what could she do?

PRAY.

She stilled as the thought surfaced in her mind.

PRAY.

She closed her eyes, a new wave of emotions pushing aside the ones from seconds ago. Unable to contain the surge, a strangled sob broke free, quickly followed by a stream of tears. How could life have become so twisted? Was it that long ago she had bemoaned her mundane life? What she wouldn't give to have that life back now.

She hugged herself as the emotions continued to run free. It was too much. Why would God let Emery be forced into marriage? Why would He let her escape only to get hurt? Earlier her turn of events had seemed like a God thing, but now she wasn't sure.

Her thoughts continued to spiral downward, dragging her down with them. Just when she felt the wave about to overtake her, a story from the Bible came to mind.

She paused, contemplating the story of Joseph. She remembered Joseph had been sold into slavery by his brothers and later in Egypt was accused of something he didn't do and thrown into prison. Something about the prison part pricked her memory. She concentrated, trying to recall the details. Then, it hit her – the dream interpretation.

She remembered Joseph interpreted dreams for two people in Pharaoh's service while in prison. He had asked them to remember him if they were returned to service for Pharaoh. One of them was soon returned to service but forgot about Joseph until a few years later.

She reflected on how Joseph must have felt. Like her, he was probably optimistic things were starting to turn around for the better, but then the man forgot him. Had he been angry at God? Had he questioned why?

No sooner after pondering these questions, the rest of Joseph's story played through her mind. As it did, she felt her frustration slowly leak away like a deflating balloon. When Joseph finally obtained his freedom, he was placed second in command to Pharaoh and later saved many from famine, including his own family. God had delayed Joseph's freedom for a reason, for a greater purpose.

Anna closed her eyes. Could He be doing the same now? Was there something further off she couldn't see yet? But what if there's nothing else later? Not knowing what else to do, she bowed her head. No words came out. She simply sat there, unable to steer through her battling emotions.

After a while, she slowly lifted her head and dried her eyes. She looked out the window. The sun's golden glow gave the yard the appearance of an emerald sea. She breathed in the sweet fragrance around her. Sweeping her gaze over the various plants and flowers inhabiting the greenhouse, she couldn't deny the beauty found in nature. Could He bring beauty from her mess too?

Suddenly, she heard rustling nearby. Hunching lower in the chair, she held her breath. The rustling drew closer. She tensed as the greenhouse door eased open, a shadow falling across the floor. Her heart galloped in her chest. She hoped whoever it was didn't look to the left. When the figure stepped fully into the open, she couldn't keep a cry from escaping.

Everett

Thirty minutes after his almost wedding Everett found himself sitting in a car beside his father as they drove along. He had seen his father upset before, but not like this. He knew there was no reasoning with his father when he was in a mood, especially one resembling a volcano waiting to erupt.

As he looked out the window, he let his mind wander. He had come home late Thursday night to the news the wedding was being moved to Friday morning. When he asked why, his father had simply said there was no need to wait. He knew there was more to the story, but his father had appeared agitated at the time, so he let it go. When morning came, he resigned himself to getting married. He had believed his future was sealed until Emery uttered those two words – *I don't.*

He hadn't been able to hide his shock. Before he could begin to piece together what had happened, things started to unravel quickly. Emery's attempt at escape had only escalated matters. He knew when he intervened, he was risking his father's wrath, but he couldn't let him hurt Emery. Any woman, or person for that matter, who had the courage to stand against his father deserved something in return.

Shortly after Emery escaped, his father stormed out of the room. After a moment of awkward silence, he had bid the pastor, an old friend of his father's, a good day and said they would be in touch later.

Now, as he was looking for Emery, he couldn't help but wish they didn't find her. In the state his father was in, it wouldn't bode well for anyone they crossed paths with. The car came to a sudden stop, jerking him from his thoughts. Turning, he saw his father looking out the window. "What is it?"

His father pointed to a spot in the distance. "There," he replied. "I saw movement in the bushes."

He squinted his eyes but couldn't see anything. He looked around and noticed where they were. "We're close to Mr. Adler's estate," he commented.

His father turned to look at him. "Yes, but I'm not surprised."

"You're not?"

His father shook his head, turning to look out the front windshield. "You've got a lot to learn if you can't piece together why we're here."

He heard the insult and challenge. Straightening in his seat, he shuffled through the past week in his mind. He might not be as ruthless as his father, but he was not useless.

He smiled as the pieces clicked together. Glancing in his father's direction, he replied. "Emery's friend was being held at Mr. Adler's estate, so it would make sense she would go there first."

After a moment, his father made eye contact with him. There was no smile of approval or statement of good job, but he saw a hint of respect in his eyes. Turning back to the window, his father stared silently into the distance. After a few minutes, he spoke. "I think we need to split up."

"Why?"

His father adjusted his grip on the steering wheel before turning to look at him. "I want to ensure we don't miss Emery. The movement

I thought I saw is near the Adler estate, which could mean she's not there yet, or it could be her friend."

"Her friend?" he asked. "The one who was poisoned?"

His father nodded. "Yes, I received word Thursday night she had escaped and one of the staff was missing too. I'm guessing they're in cahoots together."

Emery's friend being on the loose certainly explained the wedding being moved up suddenly, but something wasn't adding up. "How can her friend be missing if she's been poisoned for the past week? Shouldn't she be too weak?"

He saw the knuckles on his father's hand turn white as his voice tightened. "Yes, that part is a mystery. Even if the missing staff member went along to help her, mentally she shouldn't have been with it enough to comprehend anything. Which begs the question, how did she know something was wrong?"

He watched the storm brewing in his father's eyes. He pitied whoever was behind their escape. His father turned back to him. "Here's what I want you to do," he said. "You will go to the Adler's estate and wait for me there. I will start here where I saw movement and make my way towards you."

He nodded and started to make his way out of the car when his father's voice made him pause. "Son, don't disappoint me in this."

He met his father's strong gaze. His look conveyed there was no room for error. He nodded again and opened the door, letting it close quietly after him, and set off in the direction of the Adler estate.

Ella

Ella felt a hitch in her side shortly after they set off again. She hadn't considered herself out of shape, but the trek through town and ducking in and out of shrubbery made her rethink her initial assessment. Looking over at Emery though quieted her complaints, at least she wasn't hampered by a wedding dress.

As they went along, her mind drifted back to the past hour. She hadn't been sure her plan would work, or if Emery would be able to read what she had written. When she had seen Emery's look of recognition, she had almost cried in relief. She hoped Anna wouldn't mind she had written on the inside cover of her Bible.

She came to an abrupt stop. Emery stopped a few paces ahead and turned back. "What is it?" she asked.

Ella looked at her, trying not to panic. "I just realized I don't have Anna's bag with her Bible and clothes in it."

Emery looked around them. "Do you think you dropped it?"

She thought back, shaking her head. "No, I don't think so. I don't remember carrying anything heavy when we started off again. I must have left it back where we rested." She glanced back in the direction they had come but decided against it. It wasn't worth it with Mr. Sterling on their tail. She was sure Anna would understand.

Facing forward again, she started walking. "Come on," she motioned to Emery. "We're almost there."

Chapter 20

Anna

Anna felt tears fall down her cheeks at the sight before her. She opened her arms as Emery fell beside her, engulfing her in an embrace. They laughed and cried as they clung to each other. They held each other for a long time before finally letting go.

When she got her first good look at Emery, her eyes grew big. "You're in a wedding dress!"

Emery glanced down before chuckling. "I almost forgot I was wearing it," she said. "It's been such a whirlwind."

She clasped her friend's hand. "Once we get out of here, you'll have to tell me everything."

"That may be a problem."

Anna looked behind her friend and noticed Ella for the first time. "What do you mean?" she asked.

"I saw movement nearby. I don't think it was Mr. Sterling…" Ella's voice trailed off as she looked out the door's window.

Anna let her gaze roll over their surroundings, straining her ears to listen. Just when she was beginning to think Ella might have been mistaken, the soft pad of footsteps reached her ears.

Ella hurried over. "It's Mr. Sterling's son," she whispered. "What should we do?"

"Maybe we could rush at him as soon as he walks in," Anna replied. "Then we could overpower him."

Emery shook her head. "He's too strong."

"What other choice do we have?" Anna asked, the footfalls urging her mind to think of something, anything.

Just then, the footsteps stopped. Anna held her breath, wishing once again she wasn't injured. After a few seconds, the door slowly started to creep open.

Everett

Everett surveyed the scene before him. Emery still wore the wedding dress, but it was much worse for wear. Dirt and leaves were pasted haphazardly over it. Her hair lay in disarray around her shoulders, and her cheeks sported red splotches. Her eyes regarded him cautiously.

Ignoring the guilt trying to surface, he turned his attention to the people beside Emery. He studied the one on her left. She glared back at him. Her disheveled auburn locks framing piercing green eyes.

Her eyes held him captive. The glimpse of vulnerability quickly hidden behind a steel curtain pricked at his heart. He shook his head, attempting to dislodge the spell. He didn't have time for this.

He looked to Emery's right and took in the attire on the young lady's small form. She wore clothing similar to the staff at his father's manor. She must be the person who escaped with Emery's friend.

He turned to Emery. "I'm here to bring you back," he stated.

"You're not taking her anywhere!" her friend exclaimed, making as if to stand.

Emery stilled her with a hand on her arm. "Anna, you can't walk remember," she said. "Let me talk to him."

Anna, that was her name. His gaze swept over her. He didn't see any visible injuries. Why couldn't she walk?

Sighing, Anna consented to wait. Emery gave her a smile before turning to him. He kept his face indifferent, locking his feelings away.

"Couldn't you pretend you didn't find us?" she asked, hope infusing her words.

"You know the answer to that," he replied, his voice stripped of emotion. "Besides, my father is out searching too."

"You could lead him away from us," Anna piped up, looking at him straight on.

Once again, his thoughts momentarily left him. Her eyes were like emerald fire, burning through his mask.

"I can't," he answered, his reply coming out gruffer than he intended.

"You mean you won't," Anna fired back, attempting to push herself up. "You're just like your father, a big brute!"

"Anna, please," Emery pleaded as she stood. "Let's sit back down."

"No," Anna replied. "I'm not going to let him take you." As if to emphasize her words, she took a step forward. Her knee buckled, and she would have crashed unceremoniously to the ground if Emery hadn't caught her, slowing her descent.

Everett hadn't realized he had taken a step forward until he glanced down. What was he doing? This was no time for softness. His father was expecting him to succeed, and he couldn't let him down again. Taking a step back, he pushed any empathy away.

"If you take Emery, you're taking me too."

"What? Anna, you can't!"

Everett noticed the set of Anna's jaw. She certainly wasn't one to back down from a challenge. She had even stood up to him. Not many dared to do so, especially knowing who his father was. If only circumstances were different, he thought. Sighing, he realized there was no point dwelling on what couldn't be changed. Best to move on.

"We need to be going," he stated, "Unless you would rather deal with my father."

He watched the flicker of fear cross Emery's eyes. His insides knotted. *Stop it*, he told himself. *This isn't your fault. No one is going to get hurt.*

Emery glanced at Anna before standing. "What about them?"

Everett looked at the other two ladies before sweeping his gaze around the greenhouse. There had to be something here he could use. Walking to some cabinets of the far wall he opened them. On the last one, he found something that would work. Grasping hold of the items, he returned to the ladies.

Emery's eyes widened. "It's the only way," he stated.

As he walked toward them, the other girl, the blonde, suddenly took off for the door. He quickly changed course and grabbed her arm as she reached the door. She attempted to yank her arm away as she kicked him. Taking both of her arms in a vise grip, he held them to her sides, spun her around, and pushed her up against the wall.

"What are you doing?" Emery cried. "Stop!"

He ignored her as he focused on the girl in front of him. She certainly was a squirmy one. He laid his broad arm across the back of her shoulders to hold her in place as he started wrapping the rope around her wrists. Lowering the arm across her back, he quickly tied the knot.

"Everett, you have to stop!" Emery exclaimed, drawing up next to him and laying her hand on his arm.

He gave the knot a firm yank. A small whimper escaped the blonde.

"I'll go with you," Emery said. "Just leave them alone."

He shrugged off her grip. "You know I can't do that." He went to work cutting another length of rope with the garden shears to secure the girl's ankles.

Emery crouched down and shoved his hands away. "I'm true to my word, so you don't have to keep tying her up."

The blonde tried to veer right, but he easily pulled her back and gave her bound wrists a firm yank. She seemed to get the hint and stopped moving. He turned to Emery beginning to feel frustrated at all the setbacks.

"Look," he whispered heatedly. "We don't have much time before my father meets me here. Do you really want him to find all three of you?"

She shook her head. "No, but — "

"This is the only way to ensure they don't follow us and further complicate things," he answered. "I'm trying to keep them out of it as much as I can, but I know they won't just sit idly by."

Emery searched his face and seemed to accept his answer because she backed away. He returned to the blonde and within a minute had her feet tied together. He led her to one of the chairs and tied another length of rope around her middle to the back of the chair. *One down*, he thought.

Not wanting to waste any more time, he went to Emery's friend, the feisty redhead. She glowered daggers at him but didn't put up a fuss. Emery stood next to her. Apparently, Emery had been able to placate her, which he was glad for. He didn't want another wresting match.

As he finished the knot at the back of the chair, he went to put the rope and garden shears back when the redhead's voice stopped him. Against his better judgment, he turned to face her. "I promise you," she said quietly, looking him dead in the eye. "You and your father won't get away with this."

Everett watched her, feeling a tug in his core. His father had always told him a man had to look after himself first to get ahead in the world. This past week though, he had begun feeling things he had never felt before. What would it be like to have such a devoted friend, willing to defy the odds?

Stop it, he told himself. *You don't need anyone. Just get the job done.*

Pivoting, he quickly returned the items to the cabinet and turned to find Emery giving her friend a hug. She whispered something in her ear before going to the other girl and repeating the same thing.

He watched as she made her way toward him at the door. As she drew up beside him, she took one last glance back before walking past him out the door. He looked back at the two ladies but seeing their tear-stained faces was too much for him, he swung around and followed Emery. They walked a while before anyone spoke.

"Will you tell your father about Anna and Ella?"

He kept his gaze focused ahead. He knew his father would be outraged to know he had left them behind. Initially, he had considered taking both of them, but he figured Emery should get something out of this arrangement. Keeping the other two away from his father was the least he could do.

"No, I don't plan to tell him," he said.

"Thank you," she whispered.

Her gratitude didn't set right with him. Here she was being forced into marriage and she was thanking him? The more they walked, the more uncomfortable he grew.

What was wrong with him? He used to be like steel – strong, immovable, unflappable. His father raised him to be indifferent to others, to let yourself feel another's pain was to weaken and lose the upper hand. Emery's voice broke through his confusion.

"Do you still want out of this arrangement?"

He looked at her. "We've already tried to find a way out."

A spark lit her eyes. "I may have a solution. It just came to me."

He listened transfixed as Emery told him about a hidden room she had discovered in the library. Why had his father not told him?

The more he heard though, the heavier his heart grew. This room was proof of his father's underhanded dealings. He knew his father wasn't always aboveboard. But knowing and stopping him were two different things.

"What do you think?" she asked, coming to a stop.

Everett halted and ran his hand across the back of his neck. "I don't know."

"I know what I'm asking of you is hard," she replied softly. "But you know what your father is doing isn't right." Her words battered against his carefully constructed wall. A structure he had painstakingly crafted throughout the years.

"Everett, if no one stops him, he will continue hurting people."

He pulled away, wishing he could do the same with her words. Her statement shattered any reasoning for backing his father. He hung his head, his hands fisted at his sides. He knew what he needed to do, what he should do, but could he? Could he stand against the man who had raised him? The one who had groomed him from childhood to take over the family business?

But is this the business you want to be known for?

Everett stilled at the thought. He wasn't sure where it had come from, but it parted the clouds engulfing him. Did he want to be like his father? Or was he doomed to become him anyway? After all, his father had been his only parental influence since his mother left when he was two.

"Everett?"

Blinking, he looked up and met Emery's gaze. Seeing her eyes laced with concern, fizzled his remaining resolve. Releasing the tension from his hands, he let his body relax.

"Okay, we'll go."

"Really?" Emery said, her eyes lighting up. "You'll help me find evidence to prove my uncle's death wasn't due to sickness?"

He nodded before taking out his phone and texting his father, telling him there was a new development. He had Emery and would meet him back at home. Finger shaking, he hit send.

Emery suddenly sobered. "Why?" she asked quietly. "Why are you choosing to help me?"

"I've grown up knowing about my father's dealings. But this past week, after witnessing it firsthand," he paused, staring off into the distance, "I don't know. Something just doesn't sit right with me anymore."

When Emery didn't respond, he looked over to find her staring, her eyes misting over.

"Now, don't start getting all mushy on me," he mumbled, beginning to walk again.

He peeked at Emery out of his peripheral vision as she came up beside him. A smile graced her lips. Part of him loosened at the knowledge he had done something right. But a larger part knew this was far from over. His father was not one to take lightly.

Chapter 21

Emery

Emery couldn't ignore the trepidation crawling down her spine. They needed to get out of here, fast. She hurried to where Everett was ruffling through files. "We need to leave!" she whispered.

Everett glanced up. "But you haven't found what you need."

She grabbed his arm before he could return to the files. "We don't have time! We need to get out of here, now!"

Everett stood and returned the files, sliding the door closed. "Alright," he said. "We can go."

Breathing a sigh of relief, she headed towards the exit, hearing Everett following behind her. When they were within a few feet of the door, it suddenly began creeping open, the scraping sound sending daggers into her heart.

Everett quickly pulled her to the side and crouched behind some filing cabinets. She tried to quiet her breathing as footsteps echoed through the chamber. She felt Everett tense beside her.

A shadow stretched across the floor. She held her breath, watching as it turned slowly one way and then the other. She prayed whoever it was wouldn't find them. Her eyes snapped back open as a scraping resounded through the room again. Was that the door?

She watched the shadow grow smaller as the footsteps faded. When she heard a click followed by silence, her shoulders drooped as her breath came out in a rush. She glanced at Everett, seeing a flicker of relief reflected in his eyes too.

After waiting a moment longer, they uncurled from their position. As they stood and rounded the cabinets, a scream escaped before she could contain it. She bumped into Everett as she stumbled backward.

"Well, well…" spoke a voice from the shadows. "Isn't this a surprise?"

Emery watched in horror as her worst nightmare materialized before her.

Mr. Sterling stepped into the light. "Here I was wondering where you two have been, only to discover you've come to the library to do a little research." His gaze hardened. "Find anything interesting?"

Her skin broke out into a sweat as her heart ricocheted in her chest.

God, please save us!

Everett stepped up alongside her. "Father, why didn't you tell me about this room?"

"Every man has his secrets son, even from family." He crossed his arms. "It appears I was right not to trust you." He shook his head. "My own flesh and blood going behind my back."

A tingle shot through Emery. She shivered. This wasn't good.

"The game is up, father," Everett replied.

"I never thought I would see the day my son would go soft."

Everett took another step forward. "You've taught me everything I know. I've helped grow this business, but it's time to stop bulldozing over others like this."

"Money is what grows a business son, and do you know how money grows?" Mr. Sterling paused, glancing in her direction. "By whatever means necessary." He turned back to Everett. "You have to make your fortune, and you don't do that by being spineless."

"You're wrong father. I've brought in continuous revenue without resorting to this," Everett said, sweeping his arm around the room.

Mr. Sterling's face turned red. "I'm wrong?" he roared. "I'm trying to grow this company, to keep the roof over your head. This is a dog-eat-dog world, only the strong survive."

"You can't keep conducting business like this," Everett answered, his voice rising in volume. "Eventually, you'll get caught."

Mr. Sterling's eyes narrowed. "Are you threatening to turn me in? Your own father."

Everett shook his head. "No, I simply want you to stop doing things under the table."

Mr. Sterling stepped forward, his eyes calculating. "What's bringing on this sudden change? Since when do you care how we earn our money?"

"I'm not sure," Everett replied, his tone losing some of its edge. "All I know is something has changed the past week."

Mr. Sterling sneered. "Oh, you've suddenly changed? Did you find religion?" he asked laughing.

Everett studied his father. "Why do you want the Adler Hotels so much?"

His father glared back. "It started off as a simple business proposition, but then things changed."

"What things?" asked Everett.

"For a while I had been suspicious someone was snooping around my affairs. I hired people to sniff out the rat and tightened the control on what information I shared with who. After a while with no progress, I began planting fake clues as bait."

"You never told me any of this," Everett stated. He paused. "Did you suspect the rat was me?"

"One can never be too sure," Mr. Sterling replied. "Anyway, I started leaving these fake clues in secret hideaways and stationing guards over them. Soon, my men found evidence of people snooping around – tracks here or there, pieces of hair left behind."

A glint entered his eyes as he continued. "I knew I was close to catching the rat, so I laid a trap. My men waited for days, and it soon paid off. They observed a man enter and leave, so they trailed him."

Mr. Sterling smiled. "It was quite the find. Turns out this man and his partner were investigators of some kind. They weren't keen on talking, so I ordered them to be held." He paused, leaning a shoulder against the wall.

"Satisfied I had found the rat, I began to pursue Mr. Adler again about buying his hotel. It was in a prime real estate spot, plus I felt it was time to expand the business to include hotels. Anyway, I noticed Mr. Adler seemed fidgety and distracted. Curious, I arranged a visit to his estate and had Alex snoop around while I conversed with Mr. Adler."

He paused. "While searching, Alex found an interesting picture tucked inside a locked desk drawer. It was of the two people I was holding captive." He straightened, reaching into his jacket. "I've kept this picture with me trying to puzzle out the connection, but it wasn't until Emery arrived that the pieces began falling into place."

He glanced her way. Her skin crawled.

He stepped away from the wall, holding out the picture. "Would you like to take a look dear?" She returned his gaze, trying to figure out his motive.

When he simply stood there, she slowly walked up beside Everett and reached out to grasp the picture. Heart thudding, she turned it over. A gasp escaped as the world became mute around her. No, no, no!

Please, God! Don't let it be true!

"What is it?" Everett asked.

She looked up, her stomach curling at Mr. Sterling's obvious pleasure.

"Isn't it wonderful how life works out sometimes?" he said.

Each of his words was like a rock to her heart, shattering something inside of her.

"Emery, who's in the picture?" Everett repeated.

She couldn't find the words, couldn't get her mind to work properly.

"Look closely son," Mr. Sterling replied. "Can't you see the resemblance?"

Everett glanced her way before leaning forward to examine the picture. Emery let him, too dazed to do anything but stand there clutching the picture.

Everett looked at her. "Are they your parents?" he asked softly.

Slowly, she nodded. "Yes," she rasped.

Everett faced his father. "What did you do to them?"

Mr. Sterling folded his arms across his chest. "Like I said, I didn't realize the connection until it was too late," he said. "Otherwise, I could have used it to my advantage."

She stared at him. How could someone be so twisted?

"Once Alex gave me the picture," he continued. "I knew Mr. Adler was somehow connected to the people I had caught. It didn't matter how or why, only that he was trying to pin something against me. I knew then he would never sell me his business, so I resorted to other measures; and well, you know the rest."

Tears formed in her eyes. "How could you?"

"My dear, business is business. It's nothing personal."

"How can you say that?" she cried. "You took everything from me. First my family, and now you're trying to take my uncle's business." Her voice cracked on a sob as tears flowed freely down her face. "When will it ever be enough for you?"

"As long as there's money to be had, it'll never be enough," he replied.

She straightened, using one hand to wipe her cheeks. "You won't get any more from me. There's nothing left for you to hold over my head."

"It may seem so," he replied. "Yet I find things are not always what they appear to be." Her eyes followed Mr. Sterling as he began walking slowly toward the door before turning to face them. "You may think you've won, but I never lose and don't intend to start now." Her heart pounded.

God, please get us out of this.

"Emotion has no place in business," Mr. Sterling continued. "It clouds your judgement and weighs you down."

She watched as he reached inside his jacket. Mr. Sterling shook his head. "It's a shame you couldn't be made to see reason."

Goosebumps rose over her skin. She shivered.

Everett stepped forward. "What are you saying?"

"I'm saying," Mr. Sterling replied. "I don't need Emery anymore to obtain James' business."

Before she could formulate an answer, she found herself staring down a gun barrel. Everett moved but stopped when his father swung the handgun at him.

"Don't come any further," Mr. Sterling stated. "This is between Emery and me. I'll deal with you later."

"Father, you can't shoot her," Everett replied. "It's not right!"

Emery turned to Everett, surprised at his passionate plea.

"Don't tell me what is and isn't right!" Mr. Sterling spat.

Fearful he would carry through on his threat, she spoke up. "Why are you doing this? If you kill me, you lose your chance at getting my uncle's business."

Mr. Sterling turned back to her. A smile slowly crept across his face. "I remembered another way I can get my hands on Adler Hotels. One I had pushed aside at the beginning, but now you've left me no choice."

Her blood turned cold, her skin clammy.

"You see," Mr. Sterling continued. "If you're out of the picture, then there's no one left to inherit the business. It will be available to purchase after a set amount of time. And no one, not you or that pesky Mr. Finley, will be able to stop me."

A click sounded.

Chapter 22

Everett

$\mathcal{E}$verett rushed his father, attempting to grab the gun from his hand. He ducked right when his father swung his arm upward. Regaining his balance, he tackled his father around the middle and scrambled to hold his gun arm down as he sprawled across him. A shot rang out.

For a brief second, he paused, but he didn't feel any pain. His father used this moment of distraction to shove him off. Everett rolled to create some space. Looking up, he saw his father aim the gun at him. Quickly, he darted forward and swiped his leg behind his father's ankles.

His father fell backwards as another shot rang out. He hurried to stand and jumped on his father; his elbow aimed downward at his stomach. He heard a swoosh of air escape his father's lips and kicked his right leg out to knock the gun from his father's hand. It skidded across the floor.

Everett scrambled up and snatched the gun off the floor. He spun around and watched his father slowly stand. For a minute, the two simply stood staring at each other.

"You won't shoot me," his father stated, his breath coming out in ragged gasps. "You don't have the guts."

Everett's hand shook slightly. Sweat dripped into his eyes. He wiped it away as he took in the man before him, the one who had raised him, who's namesake he carried, and the one who had tried to kill him.

Did he have it in him?

Deep down, he knew he didn't. He may have an eye for a business deal, but he wouldn't follow his father's path. It was a line he wasn't going to cross.

He lowered the gun. "No," he replied. "I'm not you."

His father shook his head, disgust lacing his voice. "You're a disgrace to the Sterling name. I raised you to be tough, yet you don't have it in you to do whatever it takes to make the business grow."

Everett tried to let the words slide off him. They had never been overly close, yet his father's accusations still stung. He pushed his thoughts and emotions aside. He couldn't afford to get distracted. Reaching into his pocket, he pulled out his phone with his free hand.

"What are you doing?"

He ignored his father's question as he dialed 911. His father started advancing toward him. He quickly raised the gun. "Stay where you are."

Hearing someone pick up on the other line, he requested police assistance and gave the address for the manor. Before he could get any further, his father roared and charged toward him.

He stumbled backward and dropped his phone as he held his arm up to hold back his father while keeping his arm with the gun behind him. Without the use of both arms, he lost his balance and fell hard on his back, his gun arm twisted awkwardly behind him.

Before he could catch his breath, he felt his father's hands around his throat. He clawed at his father's grip with his free hand, but his father only squeezed harder. Desperately, he willed his other arm up and around, fighting to remain conscious.

Feeling darkness begin to encroach, he used his last ounce of strength and swung the gun as hard as he could. He heard a loud smack. Suddenly, the pressure on his throat eased. He gulped in big gasps of air as he urged his arms to push him up.

Looking up, he saw his father's crumbled form a few inches from him. A spot on his father's head was bleeding slightly and already starting to form a bump. Breathing heavily, he continued to inch his way to a seated position.

Seeing his phone, Everett picked it up but saw the screen was cracked. It must have gotten broke in the scuffle. Putting it back on the ground, he worked to get his breathing under control. As he did, he looked around for Emery.

When his eyes landed on a still form lying on the floor, he froze. Ordering his limbs forward, he crawled to where she lay. Slowly, he turned her over and was relieved to see her chest rise and fall. His relief was short lived though. Beneath her white wedding dress was a pool of blood.

Gently pushing aside the layers of dress, he saw her lower right leg was bleeding. She must have been hit with a stray bullet. He swept his gaze across the room, searching for something to tie the wound. Seeing nothing, he looked down at Emery's still form. Taking in her dress, an idea came to mind.

Standing shakily to his feet, he walked to the desk to look for something sharp that would cut. Seeing nothing, he moved on to the cabinets with the same result. Frustrated, he turned around and saw his father's form sprawled across the floor. Pushing aside his rising emotions, he made his way over to his father to see if he had anything sharp hidden on his person.

His breathing quickened as he neared his father. Needing to hurry, he closed himself off and set to work at the task at hand. Feeling nothing in his father's pants' pockets, Everett moved on to his jacket. His fingers snagged on something in the inner pocket. Taking hold of it, he drew it out and saw it was a set of keys. It would have to do, he thought.

Walking the few feet back to Emery, he knelt down and began to hack at the layers in her dress. He just needed a few strips. After a few minutes, he had worked up a sweat again. *Just one more cut*, he told himself. With one last yank, the strip pulled free.

With four satin strips of cloth before him, he pushed the fabric of her dress away and started wrapping the strips tightly around the wound. When he was satisfied he had done his best to stop the bleeding, he sat back and took a moment to catch his breath.

A groan from his left reminded him now wasn't the time to let his guard down. Seeing his father move his head slightly before growing quiet again, he realized he needed to decide what to do with him. Unlike his father who had no qualms about getting rid of loose ends, he couldn't simply do away with him. Sighing, he knew that only left one choice.

Until then though, he needed a way to keep his father immobile. Turning back to Emery, he decided to cut more strips. He moved to a different section of her dress to cut them. When he was done, he took a deep breath before walking to where his father lay.

Crouching down, he didn't waste any time. He told himself there was no other choice, but he still felt a pang of regret. If only things had turned out different.

After giving the binding around his father's ankles one last yank, he checked the ones around his wrists and found them just as secure, or as secure as he could make them.

Wanting to put thoughts of his father behind him, Everett walked back to Emery and gently lifted her up. He took a moment to balance her weight in his arms before heading to the door. Shifting Emery more to the right, he raised his left hand and pulled the lever. As the door creaked open, he glanced once more at his father.

So many emotions ran through him. He knew his father loved money, but more than his own son? Recalling the sight of the gun pointed at him and the feel of his father's hands on his neck had torn the curtain from his eyes, and he saw his father for who he really was. Not sure what to do with the new image, Everett turned his back on his father and walked out the door.

Chapter 23

Ella

$\mathcal{E}$lla strained at her ropes but just like the hundred other tries, nothing. She looked at Anna a few feet away and saw her twisting and pulling with little success.

"I'm sorry Anna," she said, hanging her head. "This is all my fault."

"What do you mean?" Anna asked, pausing in her attempt to break free.

Ella felt moisture pool in the corner of her eye. "Maybe if I hadn't tried to make a run for it, we wouldn't be tied up."

Anna shook her head. "It's not your fault, Ella. He wasn't going to give us the chance to follow him. Besides, if my ankle wasn't hurt, I would have given him a wallop myself."

A small chuckle escaped past her lips. "You certainly are brave," she told Anna. "I can just picture you trying to tackle him to the ground."

Anna smiled. "It would have been nice to let out some of my frustration."

"How long do you think it's been?" Ella hesitated. "Do you think Emery really got married?"

Anna's smile fell as her face grew serious. "I don't know. I wish I could take comfort in what Emery said before she left, but I still feel useless just sitting here."

"What did she say?" Ella asked.

"She told me everything would be okay, and that we needed to trust God."

Ella studied her. "Do you agree with Emery?"

"I know she's right, but it's hard," Anna replied, looking off into the distance. "I'm used to taking action, and now I can't."

Ella pondered her words. She knew what it felt like to be backed in a corner by others, but she couldn't see God doing that. Looking at Anna, she tried to think of a way to encourage her but was stopped by a noise outside. She paused.

"Did you hear that?" Anna whispered.

Ella nodded. As the sound drew nearer, she could make out two forms. Her heartbeat matched the quickness of her breaths. She tried to make herself smaller, but the ropes made it impossible. The two forms reached the door, but she still couldn't make out who they were. As the door started to open, she prayed one of them wasn't Mr. Sterling coming back to finish the job.

Ella breathed a small sigh of relief when she saw it wasn't Mr. Sterling. She studied the men before her; she had never seen them before. One was tall with close cut brown hair, and the other was a head shorter with blonde hair. She took in the police uniform of the blonde one. She swallowed. Had they come to help or arrest them? Had Mr. Sterling sent them?

The men nodded to each other before splitting up and approaching her and Anna. Ella couldn't help shrinking back against the chair as the tall one drew near. She watched silently as he took out a pocket knife and went to work cutting her ropes. When he finished, she let out a quiet sigh of relief as she rubbed her sore wrists. It felt so good to have her arms unbound.

"Are you okay, miss?"

Ella looked up to find the man staring at her, his hazel eyes a mixture of concern and curiosity.

She took a deep breath. "I'm fine," she replied, unable to hide the slight tremor in her hands. She clasped them together.

"Everything will be okay now," he reassured her. "My name is Thad, and I'm working with Officer Jackson. We're here to help."

Ella looked around Thad to find the other man had cut the ropes around Anna and was speaking to her.

"We'll need to take you to the hospital," he said. "Your ankle is injured, possibly broken or a bad sprain."

"How did you find us?" Anna asked.

Officer Jackson turned sideways to include her and Thad in the conversation. "We received a call for help at a neighboring residence. While addressing the situation, a gentlemen mentioned two ladies were in need of help and gave us this location."

"Who called you?" Anna questioned. "Was it Emery?"

Officer Jackson shook his head. "I can't go into details at the moment about an ongoing investigation. Later though, I would like to ask you two ladies some questions, but for now we'll get you to the hospital."

Anna shook her head. "I'm not leaving until I know what happened to Emery."

Officer Jackson looked at Thad before turning back to Anna. "All I can tell you is she was injured, but –"

"What?" Anna exclaimed. "How bad is it? Is she okay?"

Officer Jackson held up his hand. "I'm not sure of the extent of her injuries, but they didn't appear life threatening. We'll take you to the hospital where she is. After you get your ankle looked at, I'm sure you'll be able to visit her."

Anna nodded. "Okay, then let's go."

Anna slid off the chair and stood, clasping the chair to support her weight as she held her injured ankle up. Officer Jackson came over and helped support her weight as he led her out of the greenhouse.

Ella pushed herself out of the chair to follow, but when she stood, her legs wobbled. She felt a hand at her back and elbow steady her.

"Are you okay?"

She looked at Thad and her breath caught. Ugly memories stirred in the back of her mind. She quickly stepped away, putting some space between them. She took a breath to calm her nerves as she pushed the memories down.

When her emotions were under control, she glanced up to find Thad watching her. It wasn't like how the other man had looked at her, the man from her nightmares. There was no contempt or disgust in Thad's gaze.

Ella swallowed. "I'm okay," she replied.

Thad didn't pry but instead motioned to the door. "Shall we follow the others?"

Ella turned and walked towards the door. She needed to focus on the situation at hand. There was no time to think about Thad or try to interpret what his gaze meant.

After exiting the greenhouse and making her way to the front of the estate, Ella saw Officer Jackson standing by a police car. Seeing them approach, he opened the passenger door. Ella saw Anna already seated in the back. Without glancing behind her, she slid in beside Anna.

Mr. Sterling

Russell was fuming as he sat handcuffed in the back of the police car. He stared daggers at the back of the officer's head, ignoring the small throbbing in his own head. The people responsible for putting him here would pay, starting with his good for nothing son.

He still couldn't believe Everett had turned against him. He was no Sterling if his head could be turned by a young girl's plight. Thinking of Emery, his anger only boiled hotter. Then there was the other girl, one of his spies at the Adler Estate, who had disobeyed his orders. No one went against his commands without living to regret it.

Turning to the side, he gazed out the window at the fading light. His thoughts matched the encroaching darkness outside. Somehow, someway, he would get himself out of this and plan his revenge.

When the car came to a sudden stop, Russell looked through the bars separating him from the officer and saw another car with its frontend in a ditch. He sighed as the officer got out.

With nothing else to do, he watched the officer approach a man getting out of the vehicle. Something about the man seemed familiar. Russell leaned closer to the window. When the officer turned his head to the side to speak into the radio on his arm, the other man thrust a rag into the officer's face. The two stumbled to the ground. After a minute or so, one man stood, and it wasn't the officer.

Russell assessed the man as he neared the police car and a smile broke across his face. Finally, things were beginning to look up. He sat back and waited for the man to open the car door. When the dimness of the evening cloaked the car's interior, he turned to the man standing in the door's opening.

"Hello, Alex," he replied. "What brings you here?"

Alex fidgeted with his collar. "I, uh, stopped by the manor when I saw all the police cars. When I saw you escorted out, I decided it would be in my best interest to try and bail you out." He gulped. "So, I put the car in the ditch in hopes the police would stop."

Russell smiled. "You did well, Alex." He held his arms out. "Now how about getting these cuffs off me?"

Alex fumbled in his pocket before producing a pair of keys. "We better hurry," he said as he worked the key in the cuff's lock. "I don't know how long he will be knocked out."

When his wrists were free, Russell rubbed them as he stepped out of the police car. "Yes," he replied. "It wouldn't do to linger any longer."

He gazed at their surroundings, pondering what to do. They needed a fast get away, and with Alex's vehicle currently in the ditch, that left one option. He gestured toward the car. "Get in."

Alex sputtered. "You're going to take the police car?"

"Do you see another choice?"

Alex shook his head before going around to the passenger side. As Russell slid in, he nearly laughed in glee at this turn of events. Starting the car, he did a u-turn and headed away from town. Soon, very soon, he would have his revenge. But for now, he needed a safe hideaway and time to plan his next move.

Chapter 24

Emery

*E*mery ran through the estate, her heart pounding to the rhythm of her feet. She called for Anna and Ella, but no one answered. She looked in one room after another. Where were they?

She skittered into the sitting area. An empty room greeted her. She collapsed in one of the high-backed chairs, trying to hold the tears at bay. Where was everyone? She needed to warn them about Mr. Sterling.

She took a few deep breaths, trying to clear her mind. As she exhaled, a creak sounded from the hallway. The small sound was like a thunderbolt to her heart. Her skin began to perspire. *It's okay,* she told herself. *It's just the house.* Gathering her courage, she slowly turned toward the direction of the noise.

At first, she didn't see anything, but then she noticed a shadow hugging the edge of the wall. The shadow grew. She gripped the arms of the chair. Seconds later, a man stepped into the room – Mr. Sterling.

Fear immobilized her. She tried to scream or run but remained glued to the chair. Droplets of sweat broke out with each step he took. Her arms started to shake. *No,* she cried. *No!*

"Emery, wake up!"

Gasping, she jolted awake. Her heartbeat echoing in her ears as she looked around. Nothing looked familiar. Her eyes locked on the person beside her.

"Anna?"

Anna smiled, taking hold of her hand. "I'm here," she replied. "It's going to be okay."

She leaned back. It had only been a dream. Sensing the presence of another person, she turned and saw Ella.

"How are you feeling?" Ella asked.

Emery scrunched up her face, trying to make sense of her muddled thoughts. "Good, I think." She looked around. "What happened? Where am I?"

Ella clutched her hands in her lap and glanced at Anna. "You're in the hospital," Anna said gently. "There was an incident involving a gun with Mr. Sterling, and when Everett tried to wrestle it away, you took a stray bullet."

Emery leaned her head back, sorting through her recent memories. Hospital. She was in a hospital. She looked around the room at the monitor and IVs hooked to her. Glancing down, she saw her right leg was bandaged.

Emery tried to will herself to remember. Had she really been shot? Why was her mind so fuzzy?

"Ladies, I think we should let Emery rest."

A nurse entered the room, politely shooing her friends out. They promised to come back soon. She nodded; her mind busy trying to recall what had happened.

The nurse laid her hand against her shoulder. "You need to rest now."

She let the nurse push her gently back against the pillows. As she watched the nurse check the monitors and charts, her eyes grew heavy. Soon, the scene and noises faded as darkness claimed her.

Emery opened her eyes, feeling more rested than she had in a long time. Sitting up, she saw the sun streaking through the window, shining on two forms asleep in chairs. She glanced between Anna and Ella and the bed she was lying in. Like the inner workings of a clock, the gears of her mind shifted, each piece cranking into motion until running smoothly together. In that moment, everything came rushing back.

She fingered the bandage on her leg, the memory hovering at the surface. Pressing lightly against the wrapping, pain rose up. The soreness confirming the reality her mind was piecing together.

"You're awake."

She looked up to find Anna sitting up in her chair. She attempted a smile. "Yes, I'm feeling better after a good night's sleep."

"I'm glad," Anna responded, coming to stand beside her bed, her steps a little off. "But you've been asleep for two days."

"What?" she exclaimed. "Two days?"

Anna nodded. "The doctors and nurses assured us you were sleeping peacefully, but as each hour ticked away, the worry began to set in." Anna sat on the bed, grasping her hand. "I felt helpless, but then I remembered what you told me when you left with Everett."

Anna smiled. "I had to entrust you to God. I had to step back, and let Him do what only He could do." Anna chuckled lightly. "It wasn't easy at first, you know me. But when I focused on what I knew to be true, not the what ifs, I was reminded we have a God who cares and who has the power to heal."

Anna squeezed her hand. "I knew He could heal you. Each time I wondered if He might say no, I told myself I wouldn't focus on that. I decided to pray for your healing until He answered, whether it was yes or no."

Emery's eyes grew misty at her friend's words. For so long she had focused on what could go wrong, unwilling to consider what might happen if God said yes. And when she had gotten a no, she had turned away.

"What's wrong? Are you in pain?"

She looked into Anna's concerned face, shaking her head. "No, it's just…" she paused, taking a breath. "I've been thinking of all the time I've wasted being mad at God for not answering my prayers the way I wanted."

"Em, you can't live in the past," Anna replied gently.

She wiped away her tears. "I know, but it still hurts."

"And that's okay," Anna said. "God's not afraid of your feelings. He's not asking you to pretend."

She glanced up. "But I've messed up so much recently."

"Em, no one is perfect. But you learned and grew from it."

She shook her head. "I thought so too, but when Mr. Sterling showed up, I felt scared and lost again."

"You can be scared but still choose to trust God."

"Anna, that doesn't make any sense."

"Do you remember one of your mother's favorite Bible verses?"

Emery ignored the ache at the mention of parents. She nodded, swallowing past the lump forming.

"What does it say?" Anna asked softly.

She closed her eyes. The words from Psalm fifty-six forming before her, striking a chord within her. Its truth resonating outward in waves. She whispered the verse. "When I am afraid, I will trust in you." She opened her eyes. "Thanks, Anna." She replied, a small smile gracing her lips.

Anna squeezed her hand in return. Emery wiped the remaining wetness away. "Enough about me," she said. "Tell me about you."

Anna smiled. "It's not quite as adventuresome as your story."

She gave a little laugh. "Only you would consider my ordeal an adventure."

"It has the making of a grand adventure, and I have a feeling your story isn't over yet."

Another chuckle escaped. Emery felt lighter. "You and your adventures," she replied. "Aren't you ready for some normalcy?"

Anna pretended to give it some thought. Emery smiled fondly at her friend, her antics reminding her that not everything had changed. "Adventures aside, how did you get here?" she asked.

Anna dropped her hand back on the bed. "There's not much to tell," she said. "A police officer and another man named Thad showed up and untied us. The officer said the police had received a call for help nearby and someone there mentioned Ella and I needed help."

"On the way to the hospital, I wanted to know more about what happened, but the officer was pretty tightlipped about things." Anna looked apologetically at her. "All I know is what I told you earlier."

"It's okay," she replied. "I remember now."

"You do?"

Emery nodded. "Yes, Everett and I were searching for my uncle's file to present as evidence to the police when his father showed up." She shivered; the memories almost too awful to recall. Anna reached over and laid her hand over hers. Taking a breath, Emery continued.

"Before Mr. Sterling tried to kill me, he admitted to having something to do with my parents' disappearance." She swallowed. "He said he had captured two people and found a photo at my uncle's estate confirming who they were."

Emery met Anna's eyes. "It was a photo of my parents."

"Oh, Em," Anna said, pulling her into a quick hug. "I'm so sorry."

Emery returned the embrace before pulling away. She wiped away the moisture at the corner of her eyes. As Anna sat back, she noticed the brace on her leg. "Does your ankle still hurt?"

"Not much," Anna answered. "It's a lot better. The doctor said it's a bad sprain, and I will need to be in a boot for a few weeks." She patted her leg. "It's not so bad though."

"I'm glad it'll be okay," Emery replied. She glanced at her own leg. "Have they said anything about me?"

Anna nodded. "The doctor said the bullet tore through some muscle. Thankfully, it should heal fine, but will take time."

She studied her friend closely. "There's something you're not telling me."

Anna hesitated. "It's a small possibility, so it may never happen."

"What is it?"

Reluctantly, Anna told her the rest. "The doctor anticipates your leg healing fine, but he mentioned there was a possibility you may have a slight limp afterwards."

Emery stared at her bandaged leg, her thoughts swirling around her.

"Em?"

She turned to see Anna watching her. She tried to push the negative thoughts down, to not dwell on them. But instead enjoy the fact Anna and Ella were okay, and she was safe from Mr. Sterling.

"You're awake."

She looked as Ella uncurled from the chair and walked over. When Ella joined them, Emery relaxed a fraction. She didn't have to face the future alone.

God, help me to trust You. Please help me when I'm afraid.

"How are you feeling?" Ella asked.

"I'm doing okay." Seeing concern reflected in Ella's eyes, she reached over. "Truly, I'm feeling much better."

Ella bit her lip. "What's wrong?" Emery asked.

"I heard you guys talking when I woke up," Ella said softly. "I heard what Anna said about your leg." Tears filled her eyes. "I'm so sorry, Emery."

She squeezed Ella's arm. "Ella, I don't blame you."

"It's not your fault," Anna chimed in, touching Ella's shoulder. "The fault lies squarely on Mr. Sterling's shoulders."

"But I played a part in all this," Ella said, sniffing.

"Ella," Emery answered gently. "Mr. Sterling pulled the trigger, not you."

Ella looked up, her tear-stained eyes searching hers. "I haven't told you everything yet."

"What do you mean?"

Ella took a deep breath. "I was instructed to…to…" She gulped. "I was told to poison Anna."

Emery stared back, dumbfounded. Her thoughts were too jumbled to string together. She shook her head, trying to wrap her head around the girl before her doing such a thing. Ella didn't seem the type to do something like that.

"It's okay," Anna spoke up. "I've talked with Ella, and she regrets what she did."

Emery met her friend's gaze as Anna continued. "Ella was forced to do it. Mr. Sterling threatened to blackmail her for something, and if she didn't carry through with it, he said there would be dire consequences."

Emery glanced over at Ella and saw tears streaking down her face. "I'm so sorry," Ella said. "If I could do it over again, I wouldn't agree to do it."

She didn't understand everything, but Emery could see true remorse in Ella's eyes. She also knew how ruthless Mr. Sterling could be. She couldn't blame Ella for following through with his orders.

She reached over and covered Ella's hands. "It's okay, Ella. I don't blame you."

"You don't?"

"No," Emery replied. "I know what it's like to be blackmailed by Mr. Sterling. Besides, when it mattered, you did the right thing and helped Anna." Emery smiled. "You even braved coming to the Sterling Manor to help me. For that I will always be thankful."

A tear cascaded down Ella's cheek.

"What's wrong?" Anna asked.

Ella shook her head, wiping the tear away. "It's just...I'm not used to people choosing to believe my side of things."

"Well, now you have two people in your corner," Anna responded.

Ella gave a shaky smile. Sensing she needed a little reassurance, Emery reached over and pulled Ella into a hug. She felt Anna join in. When they pulled away, she noticed Ella's smile was fixed more firmly on her face. Emery smiled in return. She had a feeling she would enjoy having Ella as a friend.

Chapter 25

Emery

*E*mery had just finished dinner with Anna and Ella when two gentlemen entered the hospital room. Her heart skipped a beat at the sight of a police uniform. She focused on the one dressed in jeans and a three-quarter zip.

The men waited quietly for a moment before the police officer stepped forward. She took a deep breath, telling herself everything would be okay.

"My name is Officer Jackson, and this is Thad." He motioned to the man on his right. "He's been working closely with us on Mr. Adler's case. We won't take much of your time, but we felt it was important to brief you on the situation."

She started at the mention of her uncle. "What do you mean?" she asked, confusion loosening her tongue. "I thought my uncle was declared dead by natural causes."

Officer Jackson nodded. "That was the initial statement, but Mr. Finley brought up concerns regarding his sudden passing. After conducting a deeper investigation, there were hints of foul play, but nothing could be proven."

"So, what prompted reopening the case?" Anna questioned.

The officer looked from her to Emery. "It's okay," she said. "You can talk in front of Anna and Ella." Officer Jackson gave a nod before continuing.

"When a relative set to inherit Mr. Adler's holdings went missing so soon after arriving, it warranted reinvestigating."

"Who reported me missing?"

"Mr. Finley contacted Thad after he stopped by the estate to see you the evening following your phone conversation. When the butler reported something had come up requiring you to leave, he feared something was amiss."

Emery looked at Thad. "Why would Mr. Finley reach out to you and not the police?"

"I worked closely with your uncle and had my own concerns regarding his passing," Thad replied. "Mr. Finley had been suspicious of Mr. Sterling ever since your uncle refused to sell his business to him."

"Mr. Finley wasn't sure who was in Mr. Sterling's pocket, so he contacted me. I arrived at the estate the next day under the guise of a business associate wishing to extend my condolences. It became clear after conversing with a few of the staff that at least one person, possibly more, had been paid off. Only a select few spoke, and the others appeared skittish."

"I hung back and observed the estate from a distance for a few days. I was about to try another approach when the staff seemed frantic searching for someone or something. Shortly after, I saw someone leave and decided to follow."

Thad glanced at Ella before continuing. "When this person went to the Sterling Manor, I knew there was a connection." He gestured to Officer Jackson. "That's when I knew I needed to reach out to my friend. I've known Officer Jackson for a few years and knew he could be trusted. We began discussing different scenarios but needed a reason to search the Sterling Manor."

He looked at her. "When a 911 call came from the Sterling Manor, that was our chance. I rode with Officer Jackson to the manor, and we arrived shortly after the ambulance." He looked at Emery. "While the EMTs were attending to you, Officer Jackson and I spoke with Mr. Sterling's son while other officers took Mr. Sterling out in handcuffs."

Emery sighed in relief. "I'm glad Mr. Sterling is behind bars." The two men exchanged a look.

"What is it?" Emery asked.

Officer Jackson spoke. "I received word a short time ago that Mr. Sterling escaped."

"What?" Emery exclaimed. "How?"

"Apparently, the officer taking him in stopped to help a car in a ditch and the man knocked him out. When he came to, the police car and man were gone, along with Mr. Sterling."

"Do you think they were in on it together?" Anna questioned.

"It's a strong possibility," Officer Jackson replied. "Rest assured, we're looking into it. His son has agreed to help in any way he can, so for the time being he's aiding in the search."

"He admitted to his father's part in Mr. Adler's death," Thad said, picking up where Officer Jackson left off. "He took us to a hidden room in the library where we found a file with your uncle's name along with a few others."

He looked at Officer Jackson. "It appears Mr. Sterling orchestrated many situations to his advantage over the years." He glanced back at them. "We will do everything we can to make sure he stands trial."

"In the meantime, we will post guards outside the Adler Estate to ensure your safety," Officer Jackson replied. "We would also like to sit down with each of you and get your side of the story in greater detail."

Emery noticed Ella turning pale. She reached over and grasped her hand, trying to communicate everything would be okay.

"I promise, it's not an interrogation," said Officer Jackson. "We simply would like to sit down and discuss what happened to begin building a case against Mr. Sterling."

She squeezed Ella's hand.

"It's okay," Anna said, hobbling around the bed to stand on Ella's other side. "We're in this together."

Ella gave them a shaky nod, the fear not quite leaving her eyes. Emery glanced at the men before them. No matter what, she thought, she would ensure Ella didn't end up in jail.

The men watched them, but Ella kept her gaze down. Anna placed her hand on Ella's shoulder. Emery wondered if it was more than nervousness for her part in Mr. Sterling's treachery that kept her head down.

Had Ella had bad experiences with the police too? If so, she could understand being hesitant. The only times she had interacted with police were when they informed her of her parents' disappearance.

"Well," Officer Jackson said. "We better let you ladies get back to your evening. Miss Wilson, I will be in touch soon."

As he started to leave, Thad stayed behind. "I'll be right behind you, sir. There's something I need to discuss with Miss Wilson first."

Officer Jackson nodded and left the room. She watched Thad wearily.

"Could I speak with you privately?"

Her skin prickled. She looked at Anna, then back at Thad. He seemed sincere enough. Maybe he wanted more information about Mr. Sterling? "Okay," she said. She turned to Anna . "I'll be okay for a few minutes."

"We'll be right outside if you need us," Anna answered, giving Thad a glare for good measure before helping Ella to her feet. Together, the two of them walked out of the room, Anna's boot making a thud with each step.

When they had closed the door behind them, she turned back to Thad, waiting for him to speak. He clasped his hands together in front of him. "This won't take long," he said. "But I feel obligated to tell you I've worked with your parents many times in the past."

"What?"

"In fact," he continued. "I was supposed to partner with them on another assignment when they disappeared."

Her mind reeled. "Wait," she said, holding her hand out. "How did you know my parents? Did you meet them on one of their business trips?"

Thad regarded her silently for a moment. "Yes, you could say that."

She searched his face, but his expression remained impassive. Something she had said had tipped him off. He had been open a second ago, but her last question had caused a curtain to fall.

"How I met them doesn't matter," he said, moving the conversation along. "I wanted to tell you I haven't given up searching for them."

All thoughts of pursing the closed door stopped at his words. She cupped the side of her head. "What are you talking about? My parents are gone."

Thad shook his head. "I refuse to believe so. They were too good at their job. Besides, their bodies were never found."

She felt as if her world was spinning. What was happening? Snippets of his words floated through her mind. Too good at their job. Bodies never found.

She looked up. "What are you saying?"

"I'm saying I won't give up looking for them until I find them."

She shook her head. "It's no use. Don't you think they would have shown up by now if they were alive?"

His face became speculative. "Not if something or someone was preventing them."

"It's not possible," she said softly. "I heard Mr. Sterling tell me himself."

Thad's expression hardened. "I refuse to believe any word that man says without proof. He's a conniving snake."

Emery leaned back against the pillows. Could it be? It had been so long. A full year had come and gone. And Mr. Sterling had seemed so sure. He even had a picture.

"I'm sorry if I've upset you," Thad said. "I was hoping to encourage you all was not lost." He stepped back. "If I find anything, I'll let you know." With a nod, he excused himself from the room.

"Em, what did he want?" Anna asked, reentering the room and leaning against the bed to support her weaker ankle.

She shook her head, turning to gaze out the window. She watched as the day gave way to evening, the sun sinking beneath the horizon. "He wanted to tell me something," she whispered. "But it's impossible."

"What's impossible?" Ella questioned, joining them.

She continued to stare out the window, not wanting to voice her conversation with Thad for fear of getting her hopes up or reliving the pain of the past year all over again. Turning, she found her friends looking at her with concern. She attempted a smile. "Let's forget about it for now," she said. "How about we watch something on TV?"

As Anna turned the TV on, she tried to bury Thad's words. It was best to forget the whole thing.

Emery stirred. She opened her eyes, wondering what had woken her. Looking around, she saw Anna asleep on the couch against the far wall and noticed Ella had pushed two chairs together to make a bed. Seeing them, she thought of all they had been through.

There was a time she had despaired of ever seeing Anna again, fearful she would lose the last connection to her past. But God had answered her prayers through Ella, freeing not only them but Ella from Mr. Sterling's grasp.

She thought of all the times she had tried to fix the situation herself, but it had only left her more frustrated and alone. She glanced at her leg. Things may not have ended the way she envisioned, but her prayers had been answered. God had shown up in His timing and in His way.

She thought of Everett and Mr. Sterling. What did their future hold? How did she fit in it? Her mind drifted to the estate. What was she going to do with it, or with her uncle's business? And what of her parents? Could Thad be right in his belief? When the weeks had turned into months with no news, she had come to accept the truth her parents were gone. Could Mr. Sterling have lied?

Looking up, she saw the moon shining down, its illuminating glow blanketing the room in a soft light. Nothing stirred. All remained still, calm, serene. The quietness acted like a balm to her tumbling thoughts. She closed her eyes and simply listened.

After a while, a verse tickled the edges of her consciousness. Concentrating, she tried to recall it. Slowly, it began to take form. She smiled.

Opening her eyes, she considered the scene before her as the verse flowed through her mind, seeping deep inside her. It was as if God's still small voice was whispering in the silence to her. She realized then He had been whispering all along. Whispers of love and hope. Whispers of trust.

Epilogue

Emery wandered through the estate, not ready to call it a night. After nearly three months since being released from the hospital, her uncle's place felt more like home than it had before, making it harder to know what to do.

Now that the dust had settled, she needed to make a decision about her uncle's business and estate. Anna was in favor of staying, and as more days passed, she was inclined to do the same. There was something about this place that made her feel as if she belonged.

Finding herself at the library, she pushed the door open and walked in, needing a distraction from her wandering thoughts. She breathed in the scent of old paper, letting it wash over her.

Opening her eyes, she made her way to the window on the far wall. She gazed outside, watching the dusk lure the world into sleep. The sereness of the moment soothed her. After a while, her eyes grew heavy. Turning to head to her room, she paused when movement caught her eye. Squinting, she leaned her head against the glass. There it was again!

She focused on the bushes, trying to make out the shape. The closer it crept, the less it looked like an animal.

Please God, she prayed. *I can't take any more surprises.*

She willed herself not to panic as questions raced through her mind. Had Mr. Sterling found her? Was it one of his henchmen?

Thad had interviewed and checked the background of her uncle's staff before she returned to the estate with Anna and Ella. A few had left, she wasn't sure whether by choice or Thad's decision, but now she found herself second guessing the staff. Had one of them betrayed her again?

Looking back out the window, she found she was unable to tear her eyes away. She tracked the shadow's movement and watched it break into two blobs. She pressed her palms against the glass. She strained to get a better look. The figures stopped behind the last bush, hesitating only a moment, before darting across the open lawn.

She felt her world stop. It couldn't be. Her eyes had to be playing tricks on her. She sat back, dazed. It didn't make sense. She was just tired after a long day. Yet, she couldn't deny the glimpse of familiarity.

She glanced back outside, just in time to see the pair of shadows round the corner. Were they headed for the front? She stood, staggering slightly before regaining her balance. What should she do? Should she wake Anna or Ella? Should she alert Thad?

With Mr. Sterling still on the loose, Thad had been placed in charge of their safety. But today he had received a tip about something and had taken off, saying he would be back by evening. Was he back? If so, had he noticed what she had just now?

Unable to deny a sense of urgency, she turned and hurried out the library doors. Her heartbeat pounded in time with her steps as she rounded the corner and took the stairs two at a time.

Her breathing coming out in ragged gasps, she hobbled to the front window, her right leg beginning to ache. She rubbed her calf as she knelt to peek through the crack in the curtains.

For a few seconds, she simply knelt before the window, searching the front lawn for any sign of movement and working to get her breathing under control. She was about to try another outlook when a shadow crossed the walkway off to the left. Shrinking back, she shifted to get a better angle. A second shadow joined the first. They were definitely people.

As they crept nearer, the sense of familiarity returned. Something about the shape and way they walked. She gripped the windowsill. How? How was this possible?

Unable to tear her gaze away, she watched as the pair stopped within a hundred feet of the front door, hunkering down behind a nearby shrub. Goosebumps rose across her body, the hair on her arms standing at attention. Did they see her? Could they sense they were being watched?

She slowly backed away from the window, her leg a dull throb. She glanced towards the door, then back to the window. Looking again at the door, she took a small step, followed by another. Step by step, she inched her way to the front door. She grasped the handle. *Am I really doing this?* She thought. *What if I'm wrong?*

But what if you're right, another part of her questioned. She couldn't let this moment pass without finding out. Closing her eyes, she prayed for God to go before her. Then slowly, she opened her eyes and unlocked the deadbolt. Taking a deep breath, she gently tugged the door open.

Peeking around the corner, her eyes swept across the front lawn. Nothing stirred. She zeroed in on the bush she had last seen the shadowy figures. *If only I could get a better look*, she thought.

Then, as if summoned, the cloud cover parted, and the moon's silver rays shown down. Smiling, she said a prayer of thanks.

Filled with renewed hope, she took a tentative step, ignoring the stiffness forming in her lower calf. Focusing on the bush, she thought she detected a thicker layer of darkness behind it. Her heart began beating faster. Needing to know, she stepped fully away from the door, and waited.

After a moment, the darkness separated from the bush and morphed into two people. They walked around the bush and began making their way up the lane. As she watched, every muscle tensed. When they were halfway to her, the moon's light illuminated their forms.

Tears filled her eyes. A torrent of emotions coursed through her, locking her in place. What she had yearned for so long was now a vision come to life – literally.

The figures stopped at the bottom of the steps. Seeing them up close snapped her out of her trance. She ran down the steps, oblivious of her leg, never taking her eyes off the figures before her.

Breathing heavily, she stumbled to a stop at the last step. Her tears flowed freely, matching the ones streaking down their faces. Then she heard her name spoken in a voice she had missed for so long.

"Emery."

Discussion Questions

Emery found herself questioning her faith and taking a step back in her time with God after she lost her parents. Her walk with God wasn't the same afterwards. How do you respond when trials come? Have you had times of doubt?

As unwanted circumstances keep occurring for Emery, she wished for how things used to be. How does your focus affect your response? What do you see more – the mountain of problems or God? Do you spend more time looking back or looking forward?

Numerous times Emery wrestled with the why behind her troubles. Have you ever asked God why? How can difficult circumstances help draw you closer to God? What struggle, situation, or person can you give over to God today?

Throughout her journey, Emery's faith is stretched and strengthened. How has your spiritual walk changed over time? What events or people have contributed to these changes? How does it feel during times of growth?

In the end, Emery learns regardless of external circumstances, she can choose to trust God and believe the truth she knows to be true. Have you ever been driven by emotion or caught up in what you see instead of focusing on the truth found in Scripture? What does it mean to walk by faith?

Anna struggles with wanting to fix her friend's situation but is unable to do anything. Have you been in a similar situation? What are some ways you can show someone you care?

Ella has past experiences she would rather forget, yet she can't quite displace them from her mind. Do you have things from your past you wish you could do over? What does God think about your past mistakes?

Ella struggles with feelings of unworthiness. Who determines your worthiness? What steps can you take to fill your mind with God's truth about you?

Mr. Sterling is driven by money and the quest for more. Is it wrong to have wealth? Where should our security ultimately lie?

To achieve his desires, Mr. Sterling hurts others in the process and seeks the fast track in meeting his goal. Have you been hurt or shunned by others in their race up the ladder? When presented with the opportunity to take a shortcut, how should you respond?

Everett is aware of his father's underhanded means, but for a long time turns a blind eye to it. When you notice injustice, how do you respond?

In the end, Everett takes a stand against his father. Have you had to stand up for your personal beliefs, even if it meant your family or friends may ridicule you?

Which character do you relate to the most and why? What experiences in your life could be beneficial to someone else?

Backstory

This story started as a cool idea to one day see my book on a shelf, but soon turned into a journey of faith and discovery. I settled on the theme of trust after the word 'trust' kept popping up wherever I went. It was something I knew I needed to work on, so it made sense to make it the central message. Little did I know the journey such a verse would take me on.

The further I immersed myself into the story, the more Emery morphed into a mirror image of myself. At times writing was therapeutic, and other times convicting. I wanted the story to be authentic, so I knew I had to be honest with my feelings, to be vulnerable – not exactly my strong suit.

I felt like I was making progress in learning to trust God more as I neared the end of my first draft. When I finished, I entered a contest. Nothing came from the contest, but shortly after things took a dip. It was like all the pent-up emotion and stress of trying to finish the book in time for the contest caused my system to crash. It was then I learned I had anxiety.

It felt like a blow. I had just finished a book about trust, and now my world was turning upside down again. As someone who likes to be in control, the emotional aspects of my new reality made me feel helpless.

For a while, I didn't revisit my first draft. Then I came across another contest and decided to try and enter it. I revised a few pages and submitted them, hopeful and weary of what might happen.

When I found out the contest results, I was speechless. God's fingerprints had been everywhere throughout the process, and it appeared He wasn't done with the book or me yet.

As I began revising my first draft, I felt more of my emotions being channeled into the characters, especially Emery. Instead of her starting off spiritually strong, she started off struggling in her walk. Like me, Emery had to learn to work through her emotions and circumstances and reconcile them with the truth of God's word.

When I neared the end of my second draft, I began thinking of what to include in the backstory. Originally, I wasn't going to include my anxiety, thinking it didn't go along with the theme of trust, but I realized it was part of the story God was writing.

I'm learning my weaknesses, things I would rather hide from others, are what bring God the most glory. Through our struggles, He can touch others and help us see where He is at work in our life. It's not easy to be vulnerable, but I'm learning by doing so, it brings me closer to God. I'm still a work in progress, I have good and bad days, but writing has helped. For me, writing has become a way He works in and through me.

I don't know what your struggle may be, but I hope you know you are seen and loved. Like Ella discovered in the story, I hope you come to know Jesus as your Savior and God as your Heavenly Father. Doing so doesn't equate to a pain-free life, but it does mean you won't walk alone in it.

Acknowledgements

I would like to take time to thank different people who have helped me throughout the process of creating this story.

First, I want to thank God for opening the door and helping me see He can bring purpose from my struggles. Next, I would like to thank my family for always being there and for their love and support throughout my life and during the process of this story becoming a reality.

I would also like to thank my two close friends who I drew inspiration from for the character Anna. I couldn't ask for better friends. In addition, I would like to thank Xulon Press publishing for their guidance and help in bringing the story to life.

Lastly, I would like to thank any readers who picked up this book. I hope you enjoyed Emery's story and are encouraged and inspired in your own walk with God and journey through life.

9 798868 502965